"You're the very devil of a man!"

Laura stared up into Tait's gleaming eyes. "I don't think I could ever trust a man with a cleft chin."

"Would you sleep with him?"

"I might want to, but I wouldn't."

"You require a marriage proposal first." His low voice was soft and mocking.

"I require a marriage certificate!" Her fingers tightened on a little curl of black chest hair and she tugged slightly. "But not from you, Mr. McEwan. Don't let yourself think that."

"Oh yes, I can, Laura." He was very close to her now, locking his arms around her waist. "You do want to sleep with me. In fact, there's going to come a time when you will allow it."

These books may be available at your local bookseller.

Don't miss any of our special offers. Write to us at the following address for information on our newest releases.

Harlequin Reader Service
P.O. Box 52040, Phoenix, AZ 85072-2040
Canadian address: P.O. Box 2800, Postal Station A,
5170 Yonge St., Willowdale, Ont. M2N 6J3

Eagle's Ridge

Margaret Way

Harlequin Books

TORONTO • NEW YORK • LONDON
AMSTERDAM • PARIS • SYDNEY • HAMBURG
STOCKHOLM • ATHENS • TOKYO • MILAN

Original hardcover edition published in 1985
by Mills & Boon Limited

ISBN 0-373-02724-9

Harlequin Romance first edition October 1985

CHAPTER ONE

As Laura sat in her cramped office tapping away at a piece about the exotic and sullen actress, Zara Stafford, Marty Collins, her fellow journalist, came to the door.

'Hi, love!' He looked pleased to see her, then coughed harshly and nearly fell over some leather bound books piled casually on the floor. 'I wish you'd ask for a fan,' he wheezed.

'I have. I assure you.' Laura continued to concentrate on her story. 'Naturally Tucker never even heard me so don't come in here trying to incite me to mutiny.'

'It must be impossible to work!' Marty marvelled and waved eloquently around Laura's tiny domain.

'It's not getting any better with that wretched cigarette.'

'Sorry, love,' Marty explained simply. 'I'm an addict.'

'Then you should think of starting treatment.' Laura snatched up another sheet of paper and rolled it into the machine. 'What can I do for you, pal, or are you going to take it on yourself to tidy up?'

'*Tucker* wants you, sweetheart.' Marty assumed his 'Humphrey Bogart' stance coming to stand behind her, unashamedly reading over her shoulder. 'Say, kid,' he chuckled savagely, 'this is *good*. Some blondes are brainless but you can really rise to the occasion. 'Course you owe a lot to me.'

'Trust one genius to spot another,' Laura said briskly.

'You could find yourself in line for a little award,' Marty's round attractive face still stayed admiring.

'I'd deserve it for this!' Laura assured him.

'That bad, eh? Is she as gorgeous in the flesh?'
Marty was showing considerable erotic interest for a
happily married man.

'Gorgeous but nasty.'

'You *are* kind,' Marty grinned, wild-haired and
rumpled, but with the redeeming lustre of intelligence
and good humour.

'It does no good to lie.' Laura at high speed hit a 'b'
instead of a 'g' and clicked her tongue in annoyance.

'Did you know she once made Moon Face Saunders
cry?'

'That must have been when she was pregnant,'
Laura replied. 'She made *me* want to slap her and I'm
non-violent.'

'Maybe Tucker should have sent me instead of a lily
on a long stem.'

'He could send you back,' Laura suggested. 'She
wasn't going to over-tax herself with another woman.'

'Being interviewed by a man is very different to
being interviewed by a woman,' Marty pointed out
rather smugly. 'And you know full well why.'

'Let's face it, Marty,' Laura told him limpidly,
'you're married. You don't need more women in your
life.' Marty was the proud father of two adorable little
daughters.

'Yes, I know. A houseful of women is enough to
drive any man around the bend.'

'You love it.'

'I'm like me Dad,' Marty agreed merrily. 'Look,
kiddo, leave that and run away to Tucker. You know
how he gets mad. I can finish this. Polish it up if you
like.'

'Never!' Laura stood up and dropped a kiss on
Marty's forehead. 'It's mine. And so generous
considering the way she treated me.'

'The thing is, she's turned forty,' Marty explained.
'Poor soul!'

'She told me she was thirty-six,' Laura turned at the
door.

'A fortieth birthday is a time for great distress. For a woman. I have a friend who's been thirty-eight for years.' Marty sat down and picked up a re-rite cartridge. 'I'll correct your few little errors.'

'Thanks, Marty. You're a good friend. If Sue hadn't married you, I think I'd consider marrying you myself.'

'Not you, sweetheart,' Marty called after her. 'You're destined for the big time.'

In fact Marty was always making that startling observation and Laura had never ceased to be surprised by it. She was having enough difficulty making ends meet without launching into the 'big time'.

'Sit down, Kenmore,' Tucker told her, not at all politely. Tucker was possibly the most effective editor *Collage* had ever had but for all his special abilities few of the staff regarded him with liking. His manner was too abrasive and Laura was sure a medical test would find not one soft bone in his body. Moreover, he had a way of looking at a woman she didn't enjoy.

'Thank you,' she said gracefully, although she felt more like kicking him.

'That piece on Zara Stafford finished yet?' He speared his short fingers into his thinning hair.

'Almost.'

'Trivia, I'll bet.'

'I don't see what else it could be given Miz Stafford.'

'Women are so fundamentally bitchy,' Tucker growled. 'You look like a princess yet you've got claws.'

'They don't show in the article,' Laura said. 'I'm rather sorry I said that, but Zara Stafford didn't try to make it easy for me. I suspect she's a whole lot nicer to men.'

'I wanted the job done,' Tucker said. 'Anyway you seem to turn even trivia into some kind of a scoop.'

Tucker so rarely praised anyone Laura couldn't be sure whether to believe her ears.

'How is that young brother of yours?'

'Fine.' Laura looked her surprise. Tucker wasn't one to inquire about families either.

'Keeping him in boarding school must take a good slice of your pay?'

'Whatever the sacrifice he's worth it.' In her mind's eye Laura could see her brother's handsome young face, the thick, silver-gilt hair, shining grey eyes, engaging wide smile and her own face softened magically with love. 'Fourteen.' Her voice was soft and velvety with an inbuilt smile. 'He wants to be a surgeon just like our father.'

'Yeah . . .' Tucker was studying her closely without really listening to what she was saying. She was beautiful and intelligent and obviously dependent upon her good salary, yet he knew there were some things she wouldn't do. He plunged in right away.

'What do you know about Lorne Sutton?'

'The artist?'

'So you know that much. What else?'

'That he was involved in some terrible accident. His wife and his agent . . .'

'That's right they were killed,' Tucker gazed back at her with dull, blue eyes. 'As it happens it was rumoured the wife and the agent were having an affair.'

Laura showed her distaste. 'There are always rumours about newsworthy people. Most of them untrue. I've seen several of Sutton's paintings and of course I've seen photographs and read articles about him. He always seemed to me more a great big social success, you know highly saleable, than impressive or important. I expect moving in high society helps and having the kind of "star" quality people like. He's certainly very handsome in a Byronic kind of way. Losing his wife and his friend must have been a great tragedy. I suppose few of us emerge without being dealt some terrible blow by life.' Like losing one's mother and father and having to live through the misery.

'In any event he seems to have turned into a recluse.'

'It's understandable,' Laura said, shaking her head. 'They were always so much in the public eye. The magic couple everyone wanted to look at. A whole lot of publicity helps. I'm sure I remember reading they had a little boy. I think I could turn up the article in the files.'

'Don't bother, it's all here.' Tucker reached for a thick file in the top drawer of his desk and handed it to her. 'It won't take you long to go through this lot.'

'For what purpose?' Laura asked.

'I've got a job for you, my dear,' Tucker stood up and walked to the window. 'A lot of people would like to know what Lorne Sutton has been doing since the accident. His story would sell a lot of magazines.'

'Maybe,' Laura murmured, 'but how does one go about interviewing him? It's only a year ago and his grief must be still with him. He disappeared so abruptly . . .'

'Do you know where?' Tucker asked flatly.

'I'm sure you'll tell me.'

A flash of anger showed in Tucker's eyes. 'You're a cool one, Kenmore. Especially when jobs are so hard to come by.'

'It's all my good training.'

'You would like to hold on to your job?'

'Certainly, Mr Tucker,' Laura stared back at him. 'Have I offended you?'

'You do have a slight tendency to look down your nose. But then your father was the big surgeon, wasn't he?'

'He was greatly admired,' Laura said quietly.

'Yet he didn't leave you very rich?'

'He didn't consider it part of his job to make money,' Laura flashed, bright spots of colour staining the satiny sheen of her skin.

'I'm glad for your sake you were able to find a job here,' Tucker said unperturbed by his insensitive remarks or Laura's reaction. She was altogether too pure for the real world. 'Three days ago I learned where Sutton is hiding out. He's with his brother-in-law. Some cattle baron. Supposed to be as rich as Croesus, McEwan by name. It was *his* sister Sutton was married to.'

'McEwan ... McEwan ...' Laura was tapping her fingers on the arm of the chair. 'That rings a bell ... cattle baron. He wouldn't be the McEwan from a station called Eagle's Ridge?'

'You give me a little hope,' Tucker nodded. 'There's more to follow. It seems there's a Jessica McEwan who writes boring little sagas about Outback life. How it was in the old days—that kind of thing.'

'Yes, I know,' Laura responded, just a little too snappily. 'And they're not boring at all. They're fascinating.'

'You quite cheer me up.' Tucker spread his hands and his full mouth pulled down. 'What about having a jolly good crack at being her secretary?'

Laura frowned. 'You mean she needs one and you want me to go?'

Tucker shrugged and looked at her with near dislike. 'I wouldn't be sending you out there to get a tan. The old girl needs a secretary for a couple of months and I need a story, an exclusive story, on Lorne Sutton. I don't care how it's arranged.'

'You mean he wouldn't know about it?' Laura stared back at him, feeling a thousand qualms rising.

'I thought I told you. He's a recluse. Or he has been since that fatal accident. Your job is to get on to the station—I can almost guarantee you that—make yourself indispensable to Jessica McEwan—you have all the necessary abilities and qualifications—and while you're there, you can gather all the material for an article on this country's most popular and interesting artist. We'll want photographs, of course. Sutton with his son. Beside his brother-in-law, this McEwan, who sounds like a throw-back to another century; around the property. From all accounts, it's one of the historic homesteads they talk about. A lot of people are fascinated by that sort of thing. I've been told as well McEwan is an extremely good-looking man. One of those guys that figure a lot in romantic fiction. I believe we might be killing two public characters with the one stone. Who knows, an article on the McEwans might come off?'

'And you've decided to send someone there without letting them know?' Laura asked, appalled.

'How do you think a lot of articles are written?' Tucker asked shortly. 'You are so frightfully proper.'

'And I could be thrown off the property by a man from another century,' Laura returned tartly. 'Cattle barons don't take kindly to people who try to con them or come on to their property under false pretences. They're reputed to be very tough. I can just imagine the reaction to an unauthorised snoop trying to pry into their lives. Think about it, I could be lynched. From the trees, you know. One of those red river gums.'

'The thing is,' Tucker said raspingly, 'in your own way, you're a very good-looking girl. I don't intend to send Judy, for example. Judy's a good girl and she can hammer out a story but she hasn't got what some people agree on as "class". I don't doubt for a minute the McEwans are *very* classy people. Sutton, too, is a very polite guy. The old aunt is some kind of local aristocrat. You'll fit in very nicely with that lot.'

'Except I can't go.' Laura shook her shining, blonde head. 'You do see it's not . . . ethical.'

'All you have to do is help the old girl with her book and fix it so Sutton will talk to you. I'm sure you'll have no real trouble doing that. You're so fine and pure looking. If it sounds unethical, how does losing your job strike you?'

'I'd have to face it if you were about to sack me,' Laura said. She kept her chin up and her back straight but she was beset by anxiety. It would be typical of

Tucker to sack her. It didn't bother Tucker in the least that she had a young brother to look after.

'I thought you enjoyed your job?' Tucker smiled nastily. 'I'm not asking you to pry.'

'It's an enormous deceit.'

'I don't think you've been listening,' Tucker said. 'This Jessica McEwan needs a secretary for a few months and that's a job you can handle very well. As you seem to admire the old girl so much you might even enjoy it. I'm sure over that time you could get Sutton and even McEwan to talk to you. They wouldn't think for a moment you're a tough old journalist. You could put it any way you liked. You are trying to break into the magazine world. Tell them about how you majored in journalism at university. Tell them how you'd love to get a few stories to get you on to some big magazine. In any case they'd have to approve anything you wrote. I'm sure you can handle it, Kenmore. You're a very persuasive girl. Besides, you have a month's vacation coming in so I won't have to spare you all that much time. Getting Sutton into *Collage* would be a very big coup and I'm now wondering if you can't back it up with a piece on the McEwans and this place, Eagle's Ridge. A lot of people are becoming very interested in the Outback. The living should be fairly easy after the unaccustomed floods. Grass growing over a man's head and all those wild flowers the travel writers never let up about.'

'I can't do it,' Laura said. 'I would love the job if they all knew about it but I couldn't deceive my employer nor anyone else for that matter.'

'I'm your employer, Kenmore,' Tucker said quietly enough. 'I'll give you until tomorrow morning to come round. I'm not even saying you could get the job. All my contact can arrange is the interview. From then on, you're on your own. The old girl or whoever is acting for her could very well want someone else. Let me advise you to tone yourself down.'

'I beg your pardon,' Laura looked pained.

'Think about it, Kenmore,' Tucker said, eyeing her. 'Part of your job here is looking good but too much glamour might be detrimental to your chances. I'm not suggesting you wear a bun and glasses but you'd be surprised how many glamour girls miss out on certain jobs. I suppose it must have something to do with live-in. A nice quiet girl is easy to fit in. McEwan might have a wife who wouldn't be happy to have too good looking a girl around the house. No sense in letting the men have too good a time. Look at you now with those long legs.'

'I'm proud of them,' Laura said with wry humour. 'I do no end of walking. Even if I went there, to Eagle's Ridge, don't you think there might come a time when I got found out? What a terrible situation it would be for me. A common spy?'

'Never common,' Tucker said caustically. 'Besides, out there in the Never Never you've left people behind. Who would be there to know you? You're not a public figure. I feel no anxiety some spiteful person is going to break your cover. When you want to be, you can be a very agreeable girl. I'm not asking you to neglect your secretarial duties to gather information on Sutton. Just keep your eyes and ears open. You should see him every day. Why fight it, you know you have to do what you're told. It's most people's experience. If you don't go, I'll smuggle in somebody else. Tracy, she'd jump at the chance. I do know you'll manage it more easily. You'll find a way to get a story out of Sutton without doing anything disagreeable. From the way that you're frowning there, you'd think I was suggesting something monstrous.'

'That's how I feel about it,' Laura said intensely. 'Couldn't we just write to Lorne Sutton and plead for an interview? After a year of solitude he might be ready to talk.'

'You're wrong about that,' Tucker said disagreeably. 'I believe he's consumed by pity for himself. McEwan apparently is looking after him as though he were a helpless child. He's one of those temperamental artists who must like feeling sorry for themselves.'

'He had a terrible experience,' Laura said feelingly. 'A year is as a day to the deeply bereaved. And if that weren't all, his little boy has lost his mother. No little boy should have to lose his mother,' Laura murmured, gritting her teeth. 'It's too much to bear.'

'Well you've got guts, haven't you?' Tucker said. 'And if you've got any sense you'll tell me in the morning you're ready to go. What's a little duplicity to a magazine reporter? Take my advice, girl, and don't let it put you off.'

All that night Laura wrestled with her conscience. The most agonising question was: where would she find another job? She felt anguish at having to do anything underhand, but she could scarcely contemplate life on the dole. There were far too few good jobs and far too many to fill them.

Oh dear God please tell me what to do, she prayed. She realised Tucker would indeed sack her. From the very first awful moment when he had met the staff they all realised he wouldn't have the slightest hesitation replacing every one of them at a moment's notice. All the past year he had kept them in a constant state of tension. Anyone who couldn't or wouldn't shape up had to go. If needs be, in the middle of the night. Tucker was that kind of man and as happened so often the monster was prospering. Tucker had put *Collage* at the very top, but he definitely had underhand ways.

Of course Nicky's letter could be interpreted as a sign. He practically never asked his sister for anything because he knew that would only make things more difficult for her but there were several things he was needing desperately. Laura could not stop the few tears that came to her eyes. How she loved him! It had broken her heart to arrange boarding school for him which left her alone but she knew in her heart it was the best thing to do. It was an excellent school, their father's old school. Much was expected of the boys and at that stage of his development and so desperately missing his father Laura could only think a strong male presence was what Nicky needed. As brother and sister, a *lone* brother and sister since their parents had been killed, they were extremely attached and as Laura had been forced to think about it Nicky had to be allowed to become more independent of her. Thank heavens one of her father's dearest lifelong friends was now headmaster. In the early stages he had run to 'Uncle' Clive, but these days according to Clive Lambert's glowing reports Nicky was well and truly standing on his own two feet.

I've never behaved badly in my life, Laura thought, yet here I lie contemplating a massive invasion of other people's privacy. She was sure she could help Jessica McEwan with her latest book. Indeed she felt amazed she should be presented with such an opportunity. She had read two of Jessica McEwan's books—absorbing accounts of Outback life when the author was growing up, and enjoyed them immensely. The Outback was so vast and colourful as indeed were the characters who inhabited Jessica McEwan's books. How beautifully and kindly she wrote of the Aboriginal people. Laura had seen little beyond city life. It would be a tremendous experience for her. See, she was losing her guilt already. That was because in a sense she wanted to go. She would be paid for her holiday and perhaps she could so work it she could draw out a story from Lorne Sutton that he would be happy to see printed. The moment might well come when she could explain her siuation . . .

I have to write about you, or else!

He wouldn't understand. No one would understand. She had to be losing her sense of right and wrong.

In the morning, ghostly pale, Laura rehearsed her little speech for Tucker, realising full well it was probably her farewell speech.

He looked at her as though he hated her. 'Am I supposed to think this is all very honourable?'

'No,' she mustered, despite herself very dryly. Tucker, honourable? 'It seems almost as bad as breaking into someone's house to me.'

'Then you aren't part of the team, Kenmore.'

'I can't believe you mean that, Mr Tucker,' Laura said, knowing full well he could see her trembling. 'You said yourself I've worked well and I'll work my fingers to the bone on anything else.'

'But you won't take direction.'

'I can't go against my own principles.'

'That's right. Cut off your nose to spite your face. These interviews are being held Friday morning. Suite 306 at the Regent. My friend has advanced your name. You're expected to be there.'

'No.' It was a warm day but Laura felt terribly cold. 'I could discuss this, Mr Tucker, with the Association.'

'You'd be wiser not to,' Tucker told her harshly. She was a very slender girl certainly but more steel to her than he had thought. Perhaps it might be wiser to make it appear he was seeking a compromise. 'Don't you want to see the Outback?' he asked, more moderately.

'Of course I do, but not this way.' Laura's large grey eyes had picked up a lilac sheen from her dress. 'I can't think there's anything more to say, Mr Tucker, if you won't change your mind. Personally I think it's a kind of persecution. I know the rest of the staff would feel the same way.'

'Principles don't always help when you're paying the bills.'

'And deception isn't part of my life.'

'Then good day to you, Miss Kenmore,' Tucker said with grim simplicity. 'Maybe next time you won't act so foolishly. Not that there will be a next time if you go shooting off your mouth. I have a lot of influence, you know, in the business. I can put around my own story.'

'Do you want me to go now?' Laura asked, knowing once outside the door she would start to shiver violently. She couldn't believe she wouldn't find another job. She *had* to.

'Finish Friday,' Tucker rasped.

Marty, when he heard, hit the roof. 'Blackmailing swine!' he roared.

'Sit down, dear, you'll wake the children,' Sue, his wife, patted the sofa soothingly. 'I've always hated Tucker,' she said bitterly. 'Surely he can't do this?'

'He'll do it all right,' Marty instantly snorted. 'The brutal truth is his methods have pulled *Collage* out of the red. How ugly men prosper!'

'I'm so dreadfully sorry, Laura,' Sue said woefully.

'Why doesn't Tucker send Tracy? That's all she's good for.'

'He probably will,' Laura breathed and tried to laugh. 'That was a wonderful meal, Sue.'

'You barely ate a thing.' Sue put a hand on Laura's arm. 'I think I look on Tucker as the devil himself. Fancy his thinking of such a thing let alone condemning you for not wanting to be part of such a fraud.'

'Tucker doesn't care how he comes by his stories,' Marty said. 'It's just the sort of plan that would appeal to him and the chances are it could be carried off. I'm not so much shocked at the idea as his picking Laura out to do it. I mean integrity is written all over her.'

'Thanks, pal,' Laura groaned. 'Tucker made me sound quite mad. I can't think I have a hope of picking up another job quickly. In the business, I mean. I'll have to take what's available.'

'Let me speak to Tucker in the morning. We have little chats, you know,' Marty said. 'Tucker might be a ruthless bastard but he needs me. I sometimes think it's a lot simpler to be a man. Men exploit women in every way they can.'

'You don't,' Sue said gratefully. 'Do you think you can get Laura back her job?'

'In lots of ways, I don't want it,' Laura said, 'since I haven't an iota of respect for Tucker. It would have been wonderful had it been legitimate. I have holidays coming up and I've never ever seen the real Outback let alone worked with an author. What I really should do,' she said as a wry joke, 'is apply for the secretarial job. Tucker has already set it up, horrible man.'

'Yes, why don't you?' Sue said.

'*What?*'

Sue put her coffee cup on the table and looked at Laura very seriously. 'You don't have to go back to Tucker. Marty has contacts. He may be able to find you something else but it could take time. No one can deny *Collage* is very popular and Tucker has probably done that but I think you'd be better placed with a more prestigious . . .'

'God!' Marty groaned.

'Magazine.' Sue continued. 'After all, Marty, Tucker has never been harsh with you.'

'He can't afford to be,' Marty said grimly. 'I could speak to Max Gould,' he told Laura. 'We've known each other for a long time. Besides—he owes me a favour.'

'Oh, could you, Marty?' Laura actually wrung her hands.

'It won't happen all at once, sweetheart,' Marty told her. 'It ain't easy.'

'I know.' Laura, who had cheered a little, suddenly drooped.

'Why don't you take that secretarial job?' Sue urged her. 'Tucker was kind enough to put your name down. You go get it. At least you'll have employment for a couple of months and allow Marty a little time to do something for you.'

'But that's false pretences as well.' A shadow fell across Laura's fine boned face.

'Let me see,' Sue's blue eyes sparkled. 'You'll be

paying Tucker out and you're certainly highly qualified for the job. You will, in fact, be going as a secretary. No more, no less. How you came to apply might be a little strange but you need the job and you're well able to do it.'

'And what about Tucker?'

'Just tell him you're going along to the interview and quit after.' Marty started to laugh. 'Can't you just see his face? And there would be nothing he could do without incriminating himself. Oh, what a perfect doublecross!'

Sue joined in his laughter a little painfully but Laura gazed from one to the other without speaking.

'It's not exactly what you want, Laura, I know.' Sue, in young middle-age still looked very girlish.

'And we're all assuming I'll get the job. Whoever conducts the interviews may well decide on someone else.'

'Well that's it then!' Marty gestured with his hands. 'I think myself you'll get it. I know you could do the job well. There is nothing to be ashamed of. You'll be applying for a job you need, isn't that true? Jobs these days aren't ready to hand. There might be quite an interval before we can find something else for you in journalism. However, I'll start checking that out in the morning. Gruesome old Tucker may have even had a change of heart. Some things are totally unacceptable though what he's proposing has been done before today. Reporters are notoriously devious.' Marty looked across at Laura with his deep brown eyes. 'Let me talk to Tucker in the morning first. I'm not a very brave man but I'm not afraid of him. Perhaps I can persuade him to re-think the whole thing.'

Perhaps.

CHAPTER TWO

As far as Laura was concerned she was in disguise. Ordinarily she played up her looks. This particular morning she played them down. None of it hid the fact she was a good-looking young woman, but the total impression instead of stunning was dignity and calm. Her beautiful silver-gilt hair she usually wore swinging to her shoulders was drawn straight back from her face and pinned neatly with a silver slide at her nape; she wore a classic crêpe-de-chine shirt and linen skirt (she couldn't do much about the leggy look), make-up she kept to a minimum and in her handbag she had a pair of executive type glasses (with plain glass) that were perfect to complete the bookish and efficient image. She didn't really want to wear the glasses but she would slip them on if she had to.

For quite a few years now she had listened to people (mostly men) telling her she was beautiful, but some people still found it difficult to believe a beautiful girl could be clever as well. She had discovered it was best to tone down her looks sometimes, especially when applying for an interview of this kind. In her early days of job hunting a woman editor, a former beauty whose looks were fading, had not even given her a chance but selected another girl who had done less well in her course but whose looks would not torment. It wasn't an idea Laura had, there was truth in it.

With two other girls Laura sat along the wall outside Suite 306. The girl beside her was very nice and friendly and they chatted quietly, but the dark young woman second in line was very cold and stiff looking at Laura in an odd way which was beginning to make her nervous. Did she know her from someplace? Had she recognised her as a journalist, an ex-journalist, with *Collage*. Laura had to remind herself forcibly she wasn't playing a part. She really needed this job. Marty's efforts to get through to Tucker had unfortunately failed but Max Gould had agreed to take her on a few months hence when one of his women reporters married and went to settle permanently in New Zealand.

Jessica McEwan it seemed was not conducting the interviews herself but a Mrs Winston-Hill, an unnervingly haughty and elegant woman of perhaps thirty who had advanced once to the door, swept the candidates with rather terrible light blue eyes which seemed to imply they were rather a slack lot, then drew back narrow but impeccable lips to order the first girl in. The voice, clear and cold, was not really a surprise and the girl beside Laura turned her bright face and made a little whispered joke. Mrs Winston-Hill was a tough one and Laura had the certain feeling she disliked Laura the most. Certainly those glacial eyes had rested on Laura longest and she had forgotten to tuck her long slender legs under her but had them neatly but eye-catchingly crossed. Ah well, perhaps she didn't deserve the chance anyway, though her desire to turn the tables on Tucker was extreme.

The dark girl emerged from the suite looking smug and Laura's new friend stood up.

'Good luck!' Laura smiled at her.

'We might be able to fit in a cup of coffee after?'

'That would be nice.' After all she wouldn't have to hurry back to the office.

Number Two was in for an amazingly short time (too frivolous?), then it was Laura's turn.

Mrs Winston-Hill looked up bleakly and gestured to Laura to sit down and Laura was reminded very unpleasantly of her early interview with that woman editor, though Mrs Winston-Hill's looks were far from fading. She was really a beauty in a razor-sharp way: probably into anorexia for she was excessively thin, sable hair that threw up the pallor of her face, piercing

light blue eyes, small exotic head held at a peculiar
attacking angle that reminded Laura of a snake about
to strike. Her tiny ears were alight with pearls and
little diamonds, a long rope about her sinuous throat, a
magnificent diamond on her left hand. She was
impeccably dressed with a perfectionist's attention to
detail, yet the whole effect was somehow intimidating.
Perhaps it was the inexplicable hint of venom; even
before they had exchanged a word, Laura was very
certain Mrs Winston-Hill disliked her. Something
preordained and automatic.

'Why have you really applied for this job, Miss
Kenmore?' she began with a strange vehemence.

For an instant Laura experienced acute shock, but
as she continued to stare into those light blue eyes she
realised that there was nothing sinister in what the
older woman was asking but an intense desire to make
Laura divulge something silly or awkward, like she
was looking for a husband on millionaire's row.

Once Laura settled she began to speak of her
interest in Miss McEwan's work. She had, in fact, re-
read the two of Jessica McEwan's books in her
possession and her sincerity was obvious. Even to Mrs
Winston-Hill.

'I hope you realise that Eagle's Ridge is a very long
way away,' Mrs Winston-Hill warned her. 'You don't
look to me like a girl who knows what isolation is like.
I wonder how you would cope with Outback life.' It
wasn't a question but a positive implication that Laura
couldn't.

Qualifications were gone into. Very thoroughly, yet
at the same time Mrs Winston-Hill didn't question
Laura about her present job which was unusual. Or
not so unusual when one considered Mrs Winston-
Hill had no intention of selecting Laura anyway. She
was merely going through the motions and coldly
enjoying conveying to Laura she simply wouldn't do.
She was even making it a little difficult for Laura not
to lose her temper which doubtless she wanted her to

do. *Why?* Surely Mrs Winston-Hill didn't have to pass the hours with Jessica McEwan's secretary? Unless she lived there? Laura felt like asking a few pointed questions herself. Really detailed ones. Perhaps that was her training. She had quite forgotten she had something to hide herself.

After a moment more, Mrs Winston-Hill's attention abruptly petered out and she stood up with almost a hint of exasperation. 'I'd like to thank you for coming along this morning, Miss Kenmore, but I can't quite see that you'd do.'

'I'm puzzled to know why, Mrs Winston-Hill,' Laura found herself retorting, irritated in turn by her poor treatment. 'I'm well qualified and I would very much like the experience.'

'All the same I don't think you're suitable. You could have an expectation of a high life. After all, Eagle's Ridge is one of the finest stations in the country.'

'Are you thinking me an opportunist, Mrs Winston-Hill?' Laura asked boldly, her luminous eyes suddenly flashing and colour highlighting the graceful bones of her face. Why was it that some women were so savage with others? Mrs Winston-Hill was showing little flashes of an almost primitive feline jealousy.

'Of course not.' Abruptly she backed down. Not surprisingly, considering the sparkle in Laura's eyes. 'What I really mean to say is I've found the girl I want.'

'The girl with the dark hair, first one in?'

'Really, Miss Kenmore, I don't have to answer that.' The older woman looked astounded Laura had guessed her choice.

'She may not be what Miss McEwan is wanting,' Laura observed, then got a hold of her tongue. 'I'm sorry. I'm disappointed.'

'You must be more in need of a job than I thought.' This with a barely concealed thin sneer. It was the only thing she had said Laura could agree with.

The older woman came quickly around the small table and began to move purposefully towards the door, which opened almost without warning. Laura thrust on her executive glasses as a form of protection, picked up her handbag and turned her head. An elderly lady was standing on the threshold, a warm smile on her face. Laura knew immediately this was Jessica McEwan, though she had never seen a photograph of her. The tall, thin frame seemed familiar, the distinguished bony face, the life and intelligence in the remarkably fine light eyes. This was a woman one could love, as Laura loved her books.

'Philippa, I'm sorry,' she said gently. 'They told me the interviews were over.' The fine eyes moved to Laura's face and Philippa responded to the unspoken question.

'Miss Kenmore is just leaving.'

Laura flushed a little at her tone and the elderly lady said unexpectedly: 'If you don't mind, my dear, I'd like you to stay.' She moved with perfect assurance into the room, subjecting Laura to a kindly but close inspection. 'I'm Jessica McEwan.'

Laura smiled and nodded. 'I thought so. Laura Kenmore, Miss McEwan. I'm honoured to meet you.' Indeed she was honoured. This woman truly wrote beautifully and she had experienced much.

'She has seen photos of you, Jessica, of course.' Philippa Winston-Hill looked far from pleased.

'No.' Laura shook her head slowly. 'I think it's more Miss McEwan looks like her books.'

'You've read them?' Jessica McEwan asked gently but with a faint glint in her eye.

'Well . . . two of them . . .' Laura smiled. 'Read and re-read them. You make people and places come alive.'

'You're being very kind to me, young lady,' Jessica McEwan laughed.

'Why not? You've given me some wonderful moments.'

'I don't think we should keep Miss Kenmore any

longer,' Philippa Winston-Hill said in a businesslike voice.

Laura, too, had remembered the girl outside the door. She would be waiting for her to have coffee. 'I do have another appointment,' Laura said.

'Then I'd be very grateful if you could come back again,' Jessica McEwan took off her hat and gently stroked her soft, grey hair. 'I believe we would get on very well together.' There was a sparkle of mischief in her eyes.

'And I, of course, would be very happy to have the job,' Laura responded.

'Then when can you come back?'

'I thought you were willing to leave this to me, Jessica dear,' Philippa Winston-Hill protested looking at the older woman in an aggrieved fashion. 'In fact I do have the perfect girl for you.'

'Not Miss Kenmore here, I suppose?'

'You haven't met the other girl, Jessica.' Philippa had completely lost her curt, patronising tone. She resembled more a fond and hurt niece.

'And I'm sure she's a good girl,' Jessica murmured soothingly, 'but Miss Kenmore and I seem to have hit it off at once. Not altogether easy to do.'

'That's all very well, Jessica,' Philippa tried again, doing a marvellous job of covering her annoyance, 'but Miss Kenmore has had no experience of working with an author.'

'I'm afraid not.' Laura agreed. I've interviewed a few. One best seller of romances who wrote copiously but dried up on sight.

'I don't think that's the main concern,' Jessica said mildly and sat down in a chair. 'Tell me, Miss Kenmore—Laura, may I?—you have the usual qualifications?' This, faintly teasingly.

'I know I can handle the job, Miss McEwan.' A clever, well-educated girl Laura radiated a natural confidence. 'It's not simply a matter of taking shorthand-typing and being used to all the modern aids. I'm deeply interested in your work and I majored in journalism at university which might be helpful.'

'Why that's really splendid!' Jessica McEwan's wonderful, humorous face lit up. 'There's plenty of scope for our girls these days, lots of options. The big gap between men and women is beginning to right itself. It will make for a better life for us all.' She continued to look at Laura with pleasure. 'But even high qualifications are by the way when there's not that essential rapport. You do want this job, Laura?'

'Very much, Miss McEwan,' Laura responded, struck by the intense desire to confide in this woman now. She looked as though she would understand.

'Really, Jessica, you're so impulsive!' Philippa said with heavy playfulness. 'The other girl told me something quite interesting . . .'

Oh my God! Laura thought. Here it comes. Her heart sank into her court shoes.

'She actually worked for *Thor Gundersen* for a time.'

'Good gracious!' Jessica McEwan turned her head to stare at the dark-haired young woman. 'How may *days* do you think?'

Philippa flushed. 'It's worse not to have worked for an author at all.'

'Well you know me, dear,' Jessica sighed. 'I go on instinct. Always have. Only let me down once but I won't go into that. Besides, I always think these things are meant to be. I wouldn't have been back to meet Laura at all only Tait decided to collect me. His meeting wasn't as involved as he thought or he brought them around very quickly. As usual,' she added fondly. 'Of course it's too bad about the other girl but I only need one secretary and I think Laura here will do very well.'

'In that case there's no more to be said.' Philippa's haughty face went cold and uninterested. 'Though if I were you, Jessica, I'd ask a few more questions.'

To Laura's alarm, Jessica nodded. She fixed Laura with her clear direct glance. 'I'm so anxious to get to work, dear. When can you start?'

'Why—almost immediately,' Laura smiled brilliantly with relief.

'It all seems so terribly ... sudden,' Philippa Winston-Hill said. 'After all, Jessica, you are inviting a strange girl into your home.'

'Exactly, dear,' Jessica McEwan returned a little coolly, 'my home.'

'Maybe Tait should see this girl,' Philippa suggested, almost bitterly. 'Just a little extra assurance. You're so kind and trusting ...'

'I assure you, Mrs Winston-Hill,' Laura said shortly, 'I'm not a criminal.'

'But you do go round fabricating excuses ...'

'My dear Philippa!' For the first time Jessica McEwan looked upset and perplexed. 'So you don't like Laura. Might you tell us why?'

'I don't like or dislike Miss Kenmore at all,' Philippa protested, now looking consummately bored and disdainful, 'it's just that I don't really trust her. I don't know why. It seems to me she's playacting.'

Am I? Is she psychic in some way? Laura wondered.

'I'm a girl who needs a job,' Laura turned to the angry Philippa. 'I won't belabour you with my responsibilities but I have a young brother to support. He's in an excellent boarding school but it costs money. Where's the playacting in that?'

'You're on your own, Laura?' Jessica McEwan now asked.

Laura took a deep, calming breath. She turned her blonde head back and looked into this sympathetic woman's eyes. 'Our parents were killed four years ago. We haven't yet learned to live with it. If we ever will.'

'My dear!' Jessica said emotionally, feeling Laura's appalling grief. 'And your brother, how old is he now?'

'Fourteen.' Laura willed her heartbeat to slow. 'I adore him. We're very close. I sent him to boarding school so he could find his own identity.'

'I know.'

'Yes, I think you do.' Laura had to fight an overwhelming impulse to cry. She had been remarkably strong for too long.

There was silence in the room for a moment, then their reflections, sympathy, distress, in Philippa's case, plain affront, were interrupted by the sound of voices outside the door of the suite.

'Tait!' Philippa looked around startled, in turn transfixing Laura with the astounding change in her expression. Philippa's cold, austere face assumed an almost unearthly beauty. Obviously she had said the magic word. Could a sister look like that? Half-sister, cousin? What was the relationship? At any rate the volte-face really worked with Laura. She completely forgot her own unhappy reverie.

There was a token tap on the door. It opened with a man's hand curled indolently around the brass knob, yet Laura had the immediate impression of strength and intensity. It was a marvellous hand really. A hand for sculpting; long-fingered, fine-nailed, indelibly tanned. The kind of hand one described as elegant. She caught the tail-end of a remark addressed to someone along the corridor . . . 'heading south of the four-ten. Should be interesting.'

The voice too gave her a tiny, involuntary shock. One didn't hear voices like that every day. It had a dark seductive quality yet woven with a faint steely thread. Whatever it was, it instantly charmed the ear.

McEwan, Laura realised with another tremor of shock. She cursed herself for having been fool enough to think this might work. That voice, the hand, had an easy superiority. In anger, he would be daunting. She would do well to truly begin to worry.

In another moment he moved into the room, stunningly, aggressively handsome with the master stroke—a devil's cleft chin. Laura stared, trying to take in the totality of the man. He was very tall (she would be just about shoulder height) very lean. Honed to the bone in fact and as tanned as a Red

Indian. He even moved like one, she thought ridiculously. The eyes betrayed him. Green eyes that leapt at you. Not bluish, or greenish, but as brilliant and translucent as the shallows around a tropical cay. Moreover those eyes were fixed on her; narrowing in a kind of recognition, but from a distance.

Involuntarily Laura stepped back, but there was nowhere she could escape to. She felt a peculiar stab of pain across her forehead as though he had invaded her brain. How could she hope to keep anything from this man?

'Tait, darling!' Jessica McEwan exclaimed contentedly.

'I'm taking you out to lunch, remember?' Mercifully he released Laura from the concentrated intensity of his gaze.

'Lovely! I wondered what was happening.'

'Finished the interviews, Philippa! You amaze me.' Now there was a curious clip to his tone, which nevertheless acted powerfully upon Mrs Winston-Hill. She began to massage her throat with an oddly sensuous motion.

It astonished Laura to the point of clicking her tounge but Miss McEwan didn't seem to notice. 'Come and meet my new secretary, darling,' she invited. 'Laura Kenmore—Laura, this is my beloved nephew, Tait McEwan.'

Laura murmured politely and gave him her hand, feeling electricity conducted from his fingers to hers, flooding her flawless skin with colour.

'My dear Miss Kenmore,' he responded smoothly with an infinitesimal touch of mockery. 'What kind of work have you been engaged in? Something you've grown bored with?'

Laura's expression changed instantly and her eyes flashed behind the owlish glasses. Sarcastic brute! There was the imprint of the devil on his face.

'You know, Tait,' Philippa of all people saved her. 'I did find the model secretary for Aunt Jessica.'

'You mean you didn't pick Miss Kenmore?' His voice was brisk.

'I did,' Jessica broke in with no trace of indignation.

'You're entitled to, Jess,' he looked at her, sounding amused.

'I'm just very keen to help,' Philippa announced with a touch of resentment. 'In fact if Aunt Jessica has made up her mind there's nothing more to be said. It just seemed to me we don't know enough about Miss Kenmore.'

'You aren't in love are you, Miss Kenmore?' McEwan asked. 'Running away? It seems a reasonable explanation.'

'Don't take any notice of him, Laura,' Miss McEwan said. 'Tait is a terrible tease.'

'No, I'm not in love, Mr McEwan,' Laura turned to look at him, 'and I would know how to handle it if I were.'

'Of course,' he gave her a slight, insolent bow. 'Above all, you look efficient.'

'I'm always much happier knowing exactly what I'm doing.'

She hadn't anticipated the way she would react to him. It made her uneasy, nerves tingling, ears ringing, adrenalin coursing through her blood. She feared, quite rightly, she might respond rashly to his provocation. Which was probably what he was aiming for. She had to assume now that neither Philippa nor Tait McEwan wanted her for the job.

'If you don't mind, Miss McEwan,' Laura said defensively, 'I promised one of the other girls I'd have coffee with her. She'll be waiting for me.'

'Where, in the corridor?' Tait McEwan gave her a taut smile.

'I should think so, yes.'

'No one there now.'

'Really?' Laura stepped forward several paces almost coming up against his outstretched arm. 'Perhaps she couldn't wait.' Laura hesitated, aware he was standing uncomfortably close to her.

'Check yourself, Miss Kenmore,' he said smoothly, dropping his hand and leading her to the door.

'She may have moved off a little, Laura,' Jessica McEwan called after them.

'I think I'll walk to the lift.' Laura frowned.

'Sure you can find the way?'

'What is that supposed to mean?' Laura couldn't help herself.

'No games with me, Miss Kenmore.' He thrust out his hand and plucked the executive glasses from her nose. 'Isn't that better?' He held the glasses up to the light.

Her flawless skin turned rather white. 'I knew I shouldn't have worn them.'

'Why did you?'

'I can do as I like.'

'Try again.'

'Blondes have to work harder at being taken seriously?'

'Believe me, I'm taking you seriously.' No levity this time, but a hard note of challenge.

'My only explanation is, it's part of the façade of an efficient secretary.'

'I'd say you were a different girl underneath.'

Laura walked ahead of him a little hurriedly aware he was studying her from head to toe. 'I think she must have gone,' she announced with a little explanatory flourish. 'Probably my interview went on too long.'

He didn't reply, gazing at her with extraordinary attention.

'I really do need this job, Mr McEwan,' she said.

'Or so you would have us believe.' Again his hand came up in sheer devilry unlocking the clasp that caught her hair. Immediately it swept forward in a shining blonde curtain framing her face in a silken beauty.

'Really!' She looked and sounded deeply shocked.

'The real you?' he asked blandly.

'Wearing my hair back is very practical for work.'

'And adding glasses is even better. You're not an actress, are you? Up and coming but not all that well known?'

Laura tossed back her hair and looked up into his handsome, high mettled face. 'I must be mad to think I'd get the job over your opposition. I think I'll go back to the room and tell your aunt.'

'Do that, Miss Kenmore,' he said suavely, 'and while you're there tell us the real reason why you have to head for the sandhills?'

'There is such a thing as wanting to work for Miss McEwan,' Laura retorted, looking up at him rebelliously. 'I've enjoyed her writing for so long.'

'So I wonder which book is your favourite?' he asked suavely, then incredibly took her chin between his fingers, looking down directly into her startled eyes.

'Oh, really!' She was in mortal fear of losing her temper.

'Which doesn't exactly answer the question.'

'My favourite book,' she told him quite passionately, 'is *Bush Magic*.'

'And your favourite character?' The indolent tone was quite belied by the expression in his gleaming eyes.

'I like them all.' Then, responding to the faint pressure on her chin. 'Perhaps, Bogie, the witch-doctor, the best.'

'My dear girl, what a splendid stab!'

'Or Miriwin the rainmaker!' She jerked her head away.

'Well, fancy!' The exclamation was as soft as a sigh.

'Why do you want so much not to believe me?'

'Because my dear Miss Kenmore, you're not as innocent as you make out.'

They were interrupted by Philippa's walking quickly out into the corridor staring incredulously in their direction. 'What is it? Is something wrong?'

'What a question!' He sounded amused and insulting at once. 'Miss Kenmore and I were merely having a chat.'

'It looks more like a struggle,' Philippa retorted, almost hotly. 'Miss Kenmore, what's happened to your hair?'

'She lost her hairslide. Isn't that right, Miss Kenmore?' Tait McEwan pressed the clasp into Laura's palm.

'Thank you.' Laura took it briskly, deftly securing her hair.

'What happened to that other girl?' Philippa now asked hoarsely.

'She got away.' Tait McEwan's startling eyes were quite brilliant with mockery. 'We've kept Miss Kenmore far too long.'

'And that's a fact,' Philippa agreed fiercely. 'If you've quite finished, Miss Kenmore, Miss McEwan would like to see you. You've kept her waiting long enough.'

'My fault,' Tait McEwan pointed out smoothly. 'I'll say sorry one hundred times.'

Just the thought brought the glitter of tears to Philippa's eyes and Laura pitied her husband. What relationship Philippa Winston-Hill bore to the McEwan family was very vague, but whatever it was her feeling for Tait McEwan was very wrong. It was distressingly obvious she was madly in love with him. She could even, so far as Laura knew, have run off and left her husband.

'Don't put any labels on me, Miss Kenmore,' Tait McEwan murmured astonishingly as Laura's eyes flickered over him in a kind of speculative accusation.

'And I'd like the same consideration,' she told him.

In the end, a second interview was arranged for the following day. Tait McEwan was waiting to take his aunt (and very likely Philippa) to lunch and both of them had more business to attend to that afternoon.

It was a reprieve of a sort although it was obvious

much to Philippa's disgust and Tait McEwan's watchfulness, Jessica McEwan had taken a considerable fancy to Laura. It was a two-way thing, as these things always are. Laura, deprived of the incomparable companionship of her mother, had warmed immediately to the sort of woman Jessica McEwan was. It almost seemed as though she had always known her, so complete was their empathy despite the big age difference. There was comfort and understanding in Jessica McEwan's fine eyes and Laura did not enjoy being less than one hundred per cent honest with her. Perhaps tomorrow she would get the opportunity to explain how her interview had come about. If it left a disagreeable taste in Miss McEwan's mouth, then Laura would have to think of something else immediately. A friend had almost persuaded her once she would make a good fashion model. Perhaps too old to start at twenty-three? It was such a mad business, mere schoolgirls were moving into the big time.

She didn't say a thing to Tucker beyond she had been granted a second interview. After all, what did she owe him? Tucker in turn accepted her seeming volte-face with a crude satisfaction in his little piggy eyes. Few people held on to their scruples when it came to losing money. He knew Kenmore would see sense just as he knew she would get the job. It was the little classy air, the silky voice.

Laura went out that evening with a party of friends. There was no point sitting at home worrying and the date had been set up well in advance. Dinner at Mario's then on to the plush Tara's for dancing. She didn't feel enormously animated, she had too much on her mind, but she dressed up as she usually did to make everyone happy. A bare, beautiful dress for a hot evening; shoe-string straps, cross-over bodice, a lovely skirt that moved, the colour violet that did marvellous, luminous things to her eyes. She even added a fuchsia-sequinned flower to her hair and smiled at the effect with pleasure. Her friends later emitted genuine gasps of admiration and Julie, not to be outdone, took her long chiffon scarf and wrapped it around her head. What's more, it looked good!

Tara's was aglitter with lights, blazing, reflecting, from the ceiling and beneath the floor. It was the most modish venue in town and from the look of it three-quarters of its young sophisticates were trying to fit in.

'Hey, c'mon,' Murray, a young solicitor grasped Laura's arm and put it through his. 'Julie's grabbed us a table. Trust *her*!' His arm moved to her waist, pressing her against him in the crush. 'You look gorgeous tonight,' he grinned at her. 'I hope you're ready for a few hours on the floor.'

It was obvious he meant dancing, so Laura smiled back. A few feet away a man at one of the best tables set down his drink and broke off a conversation to regard her, but Laura had her head turned up and away from him. It was precisely at that moment Murray dipped his dark blond head and dropped a long-pent-up kiss on Laura's glowing mouth.

'Now, now, Murray,' she cautioned him, but the tall, dark man at the table resumed talking to his friends.

Julie was already dancing a little, moving away to the floor where she and her partner soon lost themselves and after five minutes or so Laura and Murray found the urge to dance irresistible, the music pulsing all around them, lights shooting and flashing, the air drenched with a thousand flower scents the women wore. Laura was a very good dancer indeed, so much so a lot of people seemed to find it fascinating to watch her, skirt whirling, slender arms and legs moving, interpreting the strong rhythmic beat.

Murray's face broke into a wide smile and he threw his head back. 'You're terrific!'

'Ah hah!' Laura gave him a violet-sheened smiling glance. 'Loosening my feet seems to be loosening my mind.'

At the table she drank an iced mineral water,

enjoying the coldness in her mouth. It had been a while since she had been 'involved' with anyone, and for the time being that was the way she preferred it. She had lots of friends and enjoyed going out in a party, but Laura didn't find it easy to allow men to get particularly close to her. Most of them were after a good time but Laura was quite certain what she wanted in life. It did not include casual sex. The man who made love to her had to be totally absorbed in her; mind, spirit, body. She was not, for instance, about to add to Murray's collection of feminine scalps. She had never, in fact, been carried away by anyone which perversely depressed her, and she dared not dwell on the very queer effect Tait McEwan had had on her. Now there was a man who could probably write a book about long exciting affaires. He was extremely male with a considerable sexual radiance. The sort of man she had been taught to steer clear of.

It was thus very strange for Laura to see Tait McEwan materialise on the dance floor like Lucifer from a puff of smoke.

'Why good evening, Miss Kenmore,' he called to her in a surprise-filled voice. 'It is Miss Kenmore?'

Oh God help me, she thought hysterically. Tait McEwan here? She wanted to flit like a bird away from him, but gyrating bodies hemmed her in.

'It is a crush, isn't it?' His hand closed around her wrist like a steel-trap. Her skin instantly recognised his touch.

'Here with friends?' She felt her chest heave.

'Business acquaintances really. They brought me here after dinner. Heaven help you.' They were only inches away from each other and the peculiar glitter in his eyes filled her with a great agitation. It was almost as though he had discovered her in a state and place of great abandonment.

'Do you mind?'

'Mind what?' Now they were a pair and in spite of

his inbuilt hauteur she had to admit he knew what he was doing, moving to the beat with instinctive expertise, the galaxy of lights gilding his strongly defined features.

'I suggest we move away from this dance floor.' Now he looked disdainful. 'I really don't need to loosen up any more and you're too good for your own safety.'

Laura stopped moving abruptly and allowed him to guide her from the floor. With Murray or Tony they had had to fight their way through, but naturally for McEwan their pathway opened up. She thought it had a lot to do with his height and enormous presence.

'Which one of them is your boyfriend?' He never seemed to take his eyes from the sequinned flower in her hair.

'The one with the beard,' she said flippantly. 'Actually we're in a group.'

'I think you could stretch out your hand to any one of them.'

'I'm not prepared to do that.'

'Of course. You like playing the field.'

'It's my life, Mr McEwan,' she said sharply.

'You can't run away.'

'I'm not trying to.' Indeed she was standing there as if she owed him an explanation.

'In that case if you're on your own, I'll take you home. It's getting late.'

'What about your friends?'

'They'll never miss me.'

'My friends will,' she said shortly.

'Oh, I believe you.' His eyes moved from her hair, across her face to the bare slope of her shoulder. 'No one could mistake you for anyone else but yourself tonight.'

'And who might that be?' Anger soared inside her.

'Don't apologise. I just love it.'

Tony and Julie were returning from the floor, moving towards them, their eyes bright with curiosity.

Laura drew a deep breath and prepared to make the necessary introductions.

Ten minutes later they were out under a midnight blue sky. 'Okay, so you're a liar.'

Laura wrapped her arms around her curiously chilled body. 'You haven't heard my story yet.'

'I don't know that I want to,' he said harshly. 'One of the best journalists on *Collage* magazine?'

It should never have happened. He should never have been there. Julie never could keep her mouth shut, offering whole dossiers on her friends. Gratuitously.

'*Ex*-journalist.'

'You were trying to infiltrate. I know it. You know it.' Menace emanated from his lean, powerful body.

'I was prepared to lose my job rather than do that.'

'Which is your car?' he asked, ignoring her.

'The blue Mazda.' She motioned to the small car parked several feet away.

'You have a Porsche parked at home, I suppose?'

'If I could only live and work that long.'

'I think I hate liars more than anyone else,' he burst out explosively.

'So do I.'

'Is that supposed to be funny?' He suddenly grasped her by the shoulders.

'So I misrepresented myself a little. I'm not a liar.'

'You just find it hard to tell the truth.'

She bowed her head. 'I intended to tell your aunt the full story in the morning.'

'You won't have to do that any more.'

'Why don't you let your aunt decide?' she challenged him. 'She doesn't need you to decide for her. She has her own good brain.'

'Don't shout at me, lady,' he murmured.

'Why not?' She threw up her head. 'It's doing me a lot of good. You seem to think you can crack my collarbone while I tremble in fear. You're a savage!'

'You've been drinking.' He dropped his hands in disgust.

'Of course I have. Mineral water. Not that it's any of your business.'

Two police constables patrolling the beat strayed down towards them, eyeing them contemplatively.

'Get in the car,' McEwan told her shortly.

'Do you intend to join me?' she asked acidly.

'Depends if I can fit in.' He stood back while Laura went to her car, exchanging a good evening with the young policemen who responded very pleasantly. It was all so very easy for a man like McEwan.

'Dear God,' he groaned as he hunched himself into the passenger seat.

'If you will be so tall you'll have to put up with the consequences. Where to, Mr McEwan?' she asked shortly.

'Your place. Unless you're too mean to offer me a cup of coffee.'

'You can't come to my place,' Laura said, beset by a confusion of feelings; anger, embarrassment and a dark, swirling excitement. He was unnervingly physical, the kind of male she couldn't handle.

'I'm certain you have other male visitors,' he gave her a brief, disturbing glance.

'I can't have done. I'm sure I'd remember.'

'Do you know what invasion of privacy is, Miss Kenmore?'

'I must confess I do.' She was upset but she decided to be flippant, not let him get to her. 'What the lay man calls invasion of privacy, a journalist calls enterprising.'

'And that made you decide to apply for a job under false pretences, inveigle your way on to my property, then report on the household?'

'That was the plan,' she swallowed. 'In the end I couldn't do it. I'm amazed you thought I could.'

'So why the masquerade?' he growled. 'The whole thing is disgusting!'

'Look here . . .'

'Watch it!' he almost shouted as Laura took her eye momentarily from the road.

'What's with you men that you think you're not safe when a woman is behind the wheel?' She bitterly resented that flicker of male alarm.

'In answer to that, Miss Kenmore,' he said, very deliberately and coolly, 'women have the monstrous habit of engaging in other pursuits while they're driving. Do you think you can keep your eye on the road? We might at least be fortunate enough to arrive home.'

'I don't know where home is,' she said pointedly. 'The Regent is it?'

'The Regent when I'm in this city. I live at Eagle's Ridge, but that won't interest you.'

'It interests me a great deal,' she sighed wistfully. 'I have the most passionate desire to see it.'

'Nevertheless, I'm not happy to have you there. I've never read an article about myself yet I'm wholly satisfied with.'

'Naturally being you, you'd suppose you're the prime interest?'

He shrugged his wide shoulders ironically. 'I really think, Miss Kenmore, you'd fit me in. Who is the poor unfortunate you were scheming to put on paper? My brother-in-law?'

'Is that so surprising?' she asked a lot more calmly than she felt. 'The public can't bear to have their idols taken from them.'

'Why didn't you just ring to make an appointment?' he asked caustically.

'I daresay if you weren't so fearfully remote I might have tried it. I can be very persuasive.'

'Especially when you're dressed like that.' His expression wasn't admiring but malevolent.

'If you're so disgusted with me, what have we to say to each other?'

'Oh, Laura!' he mocked her, 'haven't you forfeited the gallant approach?'

'I've forfeited nothing,' she protested. 'I'm integrity itself. Everyone says so.'

'Not me.'

'Then the very last thing I would do is take you home.'

'We passed the Regent ten minutes ago.'

'You must be suffering terribly in that bucket seat?'

'A little car for a little girl.'

She understood at once he wasn't referring to stature, but character.

CHAPTER THREE

LAURA drove into her car port quietly, gratified despite herself that she had cleaned and tidied her unit and bought fresh flowers that same afternoon. Often she went without lunch so she could have flowers around her. They lent such charm and beauty and they reminded her of her wonderful childhood when her parents had been alive. Her father's only relaxation had been the garden and her mother had always filled the house with flowers. In a sense it was extremely difficult to live without them.

McEwan stood on the threshold, his dominant dark face unexpectedly showing a flash of pleasure. Laura turned back to look at him and it was gone in an instant.

'Welcome to my humble abode.'

'Your parents feel no anxiety you're away from them?' He moved further into the living room, looking around him.

Clearly his aunt had told him no more about her. 'My parents are dead,' she told him quietly.

He frowned sharply and gave her an extremely penetrating look. 'I'm sorry.'

'You don't particularly look as though you believe me.' There was a faint tremor in her voice.

'I'm far from sure of you, Laura.'

She shook her head, ridiculously disturbed by the sound of her name on his lips. 'Road victims, isn't that what they call it?' She walked across the room and picked up a large photograph in a silver frame. 'They were returning from a day trip to the mountains. My father was a leading surgeon. He had little time to relax. They weren't even going at all.'

'I'm very sorry.' He took the photograph from her.

42

'I know what tragedy is like.'

'Yes.' She bit on her lip and took a deep breath. There were many sides to this man, confrontation and comfort.

'You haven't changed a bit,' he said gently. 'And this is your brother?'

A tender smile eased the tension in her face. 'That's Nicky. He's at boarding school.' She named it. 'I wish every day I had him with me but that's only being selfish. He's found his place and he's doing very well.'

'And what happened to your home?'

'I had to sell it, of course. There has to be money for Nick. He's going to follow our father into medicine. That's all he has ever wanted to do.'

'And you?' He lifted his head to stare at her with brilliant, curious eyes.

'I enjoy what I'm doing. Or I have up until now.' She took the photograph from him and replaced it on the small, circular table. The light made a glowing nimbus of her hair, caught the sheen of her skin, the deeper violet in the folds of her dress.

'I suppose your boss suggested it?'

She gave him a pleading glance. 'Mostly I do what I'm told.'

'In that case, make us a cup of coffee. I'm sure I don't know how you stood the noise in that Tara's. I'm puzzled the Ingrams decided to take me there.'

'I suppose a man like you would find it difficult to be confined.' Laura waved him towards an armchair, but he followed her into the kitchen. 'Mind you, you looked perfectly at home on the dance floor.'

'Are you mad?'

'Is that the wrong thing to say to a cattle baron?' She swung around to a cupboard, taking out her best coffee cups and saucers. For some reason her heart was thudding, and she assumed it was because of his rather daunting aura.

'One must keep up with a few social graces, but spare me too much of it. You looked like you've been dancing from the cradle.'

'I love it,' she said lightly. 'I took ballet lessons for years.'

'I knew that in my bones.' He passed her the glass jug from the percolator and their fingers touched. The slightest contact that seemed to flash a message to Laura's nerve ends. For the first time in her life she felt an appalling vulnerability, an awareness almost too intense to bear. She filled the jug unable to speak, afraid to think.

'Have I done something?' he finally asked, very dryly.

'I feel I hardly know where to start?'

'From the beginning, I'm sure,' he returned, rather severely. 'Perhaps I can find some excuse for you. Not that it's going to change anything.'

'Do you think I like doing anything underhand?' she challenged him.

'Try to put anything over me, Miss Kenmore, and you might suffer for it all your life. Believe it before you have to learn it.' He had changed now from sympathetic to appallingly formidable.

Her skin had lost its lovely colour and she looked rather white. 'I've enjoyed my job and I've never been asked to do anything I felt I could not do.'

'Really? Go on.'

Laura paused to pour out the coffee, irritated by the faint trembling in her hand. 'Shall we have this in the living room?'

'I guess so before you spill it. Here, give it to me.'

In the living room she sat opposite him, her skirt fanning around her like the petals of a flower, showing her lovely, long legs. 'You must know your brother-in-law is news. People want to know what has happened to him. At one time one couldn't pick up a glossy magazine without seeing a photograph of Lorne Sutton . . . and his beautiful wife.'

'My sister,' McEwan added very harshly.

'I recognise your pain. The thing is, Mr McEwan, we have a new editor—or fairly new. He has ideas of his own about getting stories . . .'

'That just barely keeps him out of jail. What's his name?'

'Are you going to see him?' Laura asked.

'I certainly am,' he answered curtly, his resonant voice steely with anger. 'I just hope for your sake, Laura, you're keeping your story straight.'

'What will you do to him?' The blood seemed to drain entirely from her skin.

'Thump him most probably. After.' He stared at her. 'What have you gone so white for? What are you afraid of?'

'I'm not afraid.'

'You are. You're trembling.'

'I don't believe you've seen yourself when you're angry,' she said very seriously.

'I'm too much the gentleman, Laura, to turn you over my knee. Though I'd love to. You certainly need some punishment.'

'I don't want you to tell your aunt.'

'Oh yes.'

Laura felt the anguish of shame. 'I refused to do it, you know.'

'But you thought it only right to turn up for the interview?' he asked very sceptically.

'He would have sacked me. I desperately need a job. Right away. I have responsibilities, commitments.'

'Is this some little show, Miss Kenmore?' he asked acidly. 'Shimmering eyes and quivering mouth.'

'No, oh no!' She lifted up her head.

'You seem a highly accomplished actress to me. The only thing you got wrong was the plain glass in those ridiculous glasses, but I suppose there was no way you could afford to fall over.'

'I've lost a job before because I was . . .'

'Too damned beautiful?'

'Nice looking, yes.'

'That was no way to act.'

'All that was different was I toned myself down.'

'Don't I know it!' He set his coffee cup down almost violently. 'When I saw you walk into that nightclub I was all for grabbing you and shaking you to bits. As it was I had to wait until you were almost ready to leave. Talk about two separate girls, though I knew you were playing some game.'

She shook her head, one side of her hair sliding forward to curtain her face. 'I needed the job and I believe I can do it. *Collage* has no part of it. All Tucker did was get me in.'

'How?'

He seemed immensely tough and powerful. 'I don't know,' she whispered. 'He has all sorts of connections.'

'I think I'll deprive him of at least one.'

'I told him that kind of thing was too dangerous.'

'Dangerous?' His winged black eyebrows met. 'It's disgusting. The public have to be protected from men like this Tucker.' His voice dripped contempt.

'In any case I was finished there.' She had to be tired because she felt herself close to tears.

'I'll learn that quite quickly tomorrow,' he assured her. 'You had my aunt totally wrapped up in you. She took to you on sight.'

Laura's luminous eyes mirrored her sadness. 'I'm very sorry I had to deceive her in even the smallest way. I really did intend to tell her tomorrow.'

He laughed and it wasn't a pleasant sound. 'Oh you can tell her, Laura. You owe her that much.'

'All right.' She stood up very tautly. 'There are some positions one finds oneself in when it's impossible to win.'

'Winning isn't the point,' he pointed out curtly. 'You knew what you were doing.'

'All right. I said all right,' she told him a little fiercely, and now her eyes were blinded by sudden tears. She went to rush to the door but his hand came out and gripped her arm. 'Let-me-go!'

'Don't cry in front of me.'

'I wouldn't,' she returned passionately, her silvery eyes blazing. 'You had to know, now you know, so let me go. Dammit.' It was appalling to feel so weak and helpless.

'You seem to forget, Laura, you're due for some punishment.'

'Never.' She gritted her small white teeth.

'It's tough, isn't it, being so helpless?'

She made a funny little hissing sound and tried to raise her hand but his arms came around her in a crushing grip. 'Oh, how you change, Miss Kenmore,' he mocked her, his green eyes narrowing like a jungle cat's. 'You don't like it. I sure as hell don't, but I can't think of anything more effective.'

'You wicked bully!' She made a tremendous effort to break his grip, but even as she struggled he bent his dark head and caught up her mouth, his lips clinging, his tongue probing its sweet interior so she stopped struggling in acute reaction, her body melting involuntarily against his hard, unfamiliar strength. It was dazzling, dazing, and she couldn't seem to withhold all he was taking too easily.

It seemed endless, languorous moments before he released her and moments more before she could open her eyes. Her light, slender body was aching and heavy and without thinking she gave a soft, shuddering sigh. She had thought she had been kissed many times before but, after all, it was the first time.

He brought up his hand and touched her cheek almost gently. 'You don't look so fiery any more. In fact you look spectacularly dreamy.'

'I've never had a kiss forced on me before.'

'Isn't it every girl's fantasy?'

'Only men believe it. I hated it.'

'You shouldn't have let me drain your mouth then. Isn't that right, Laura? I couldn't be sure it was a

punishment any more. The pleasure kept getting in
the way.'

There was no answer to it and she moved swayingly
towards the door. 'You know altogether too much
about me, Mr McEwan. I suppose I deserved
something, but not that.'

'What could be more expected between a man and a
woman?' He joined her, studying her with a cool face.
'Besides, it's fairly obvious you like danger.'

'Oh, I hope not,' she said, resisting the need to press
a palm to her racing heartbeat. 'You want me to speak
to your aunt tomorrow?'

'You see you have to?' he told her mercilessly. His
white teeth snapped together and his shapely mouth
twisted sardonically. 'It might be as well if you don't
go into the office either. I'll be paying your Mr
Tucker a visit first thing.'

'Bringing me more trouble.' She put up her hand
and ran it distraughtly through her hair, dislodging
the sequinned flower hair ornament which he
astonishingly plucked from the silvery-gilt strands and
calmly pocketed.

'Just a little memento.'

'You're crazy.' Her luminous eyes were wide.

'I can afford to be,' he drawled. 'You can't.'

There was a discernible change in Miss McEwan's
manner when Laura called at her suite the next
morning. Nevertheless she sat quietly and allowed
Laura to tell her the whole story.

'Couldn't you have told me all this yesterday?' she
exclaimed at one point.

'I couldn't really, Miss McEwan. We weren't alone.'

'No . . . I suppose.'

'I'm really terribly sorry I had to misrepresent
myself in any way, but I badly need a job and being
your secretary sounded like a dream.'

'I can't believe this man Tucker would really sack
you,' Miss McEwan said.

'Oh he would,' Laura sighed. 'He's sacked four people already. The ones who didn't see eye to eye with his policies. It's not uncommon.'

'How squalid.'

'Don't despise me too much,' Laura said heavily.

'Oh I don't despise you, my dear. How could you think that? I can pardon your part in it all. You say you meant to tell me and I'm sure you would have.' Miss McEwan tried to smile. 'I understand my nephew visited you last night?'

'So I didn't get off scot-free.'

'Was he very angry with you?' Jessica McEwan faltered.

'I'm certain he doesn't want to see me again.'

'Do you know he has gone in to see your Mr Tucker?'

'I hope he finds him,' Laura said. 'Tucker deserves all he gets. If nobody else does.'

'Well I still want you,' Miss McEwan said. 'We've suffered a small set-back but now we've cleared the air. I need a highly intelligent, capable girl. My last secretary was a rather severe, unsmiling young woman. Very efficient but not very friendly. I didn't pick her either, but I am picking you.'

'And I'll do my very best for you, Miss McEwan,' Laura said. 'I understand the job was for a few months and I do have something to come back to. Another job in journalism.'

'No interviews, Laura,' Miss McEwan said.

'I accept that completely, Miss McEwan,' Laura said.

'Lorne has had a very bad time,' Jessica McEwan looked down at her folded hands. 'For that matter we all have. You know it was my niece who was killed?'

'It must have been a great tragedy.' Laura put out her hand unconsciously.

'One never loses it . . . the pain.'

Laura found herself with a mental picture of her

mother standing in the garden laughing at something Nicky had done. 'No.'

'She left a son, Jamie—James. We have him. A splendid little fellow but he's missing his mother badly. I really can't cope with the problems any more. Tait is a tower of strength but he's so busy. I can't plague him with every little thing that goes wrong. He has extraordinary resilience but the pressures are fierce. Tait does ten men's work singlehandedly.'

'I may be able to help with Jamie,' Laura suggested. 'I like children and they seem to like me. Having a little brother helped.'

Jessica had ordered morning tea and they sat talking for more than an hour. The time passed with ease. Laura found herself telling the older woman many things she thought buried deep within her and Jessica, too, contributed her confidences.

'Lorne doesn't paint anything any more, you know. Tait tells him it's better to express it . . . get it out . . . but he seems burnt out. Just a shell. Jamie feels his father's withdrawal acutely. As a matter of fact without Tait—a man in his life to look up to—Jamie would have become a very disturbed little boy.'

'I expect his father needs more time to recover,' Laura said. 'Depression cuts whole periods out of life.'

'All the publicity,' Jessica said. 'That's why he would never allow an interview. Lorne was deeply distressed by certain things that were printed in the press. He came out to Eagle's Ridge for survival. The change in him has been frightening. We won't ever tell him any of this, Laura. It would be too complicated to explain.'

It was indeed complicated. 'I don't think your nephew will be pleased you've given me the job,' Laura pointed out quietly. 'He may even refuse to have me there.'

'And upset me!' Miss McEwan exclaimed. 'Tait would never do that.'

'But he could very diplomatically try?'

'Don't fret,' Jessica said calmly. 'Everything will be all right.'

It would have been amazing if it had turned out that way, but Laura was in for a few more unpleasant shocks the first of them being her chance encounter with Philippa Winston-Hill. Philippa was walking into the hotel lobby as Laura was walking out.

'So you had the effrontery to turn up today?' Philippa spoke loudly, causing several people to turn their heads curiously seeking the source of the elegant brunette's displeasure.

'Shouldn't you have treatment, Mrs Hill, for the wax in your ears?' Laura suggested a lot more quietly.

'Winston-Hill,' Philippa corrected her coldly. 'I expect you're feeling vindictive now that Jessica has put you very firmly in your lowly place. She's excellent at that kind of thing.'

'Miss McEwan was very generous and understanding,' Laura informed her. 'If it won't inconvenience you, Mrs Hill, would you mind stepping out of my way?'

Philippa laughed almost madly, her beautifully groomed dark head thrown back. 'Insolent bitch! Is it your training?'

'Would you mind telling me, Mrs Hill, why you do dislike me? It's nothing you've since heard. You disliked me on sight.'

'Presumably I'm a very good judge of character,' Philippa said.

'Or you have an instant response to certain members of your own sex—those unfairly blessed by nature. I noticed you fell on the dark-haired girl with the poor complexion.'

'I despise you, Miss Kenmore,' Philippa said, her antipathy clearly visible. 'You can consider yourself fortunate you don't find yourself in deep trouble. I assure you the McEwans know very well how to protect themselves.'

'They're certainly in no danger from me, Mrs Hill,'

Laura said abruptly. 'Would you excuse me? I really do have to run.'

'Back to your job?' Philippa jeered unpleasantly.

'I have no job until I start work for Miss McEwan,' Laura said.

It was the very last thing Philippa expected to hear. Her light blue eyes flashed hotly. 'I beg your pardon?'

'Miss McEwan has decided to take me on,' Laura explained.

'You're joking!' Philippa's matt white skin paled and she reached out and clutched Laura's arm. 'A horrible girl like you!'

'She likes me.' Laura coolly detached the talon-like fingers. 'You seem to be in a state of shock, Mrs Hill. What has all this got to do with you anyway? I can appreciate your concern as a family friend but I've explained to Miss McEwan how everything came about and she still wants me to help her. I can, you know. I'm very capable.'

'Why you're nothing but a schemer,' Philippa said wretchedly. 'You deserve to be punished, not rewarded.'

'You can't be serious, Mrs Hill,' Laura returned intensely, 'and won't you please stand over by the wall? You're drawing a lot of attention to us with your demeanour and your raised tone.'

'Oh I can't believe this!' Nevertheless Philippa followed her. 'Tait has thought this up to hurt me.'

'Certainly not!' Laura looked shocked. 'Why would he want to do that?'

But it appeared Philippa had been talking to herself. 'You know yourself you're a fake, Miss Kenmore,' she said. 'You may have pulled the wool over poor Jessie's eyes but I assure you I'm very clear about you in my own mind. You're a sly creature who it seems is about to walk into our home.'

'Your home?' Miss McEwan had never said anything about that!

'I have always looked on Eagle's Ridge as my home,' Philippa said loftily with a burning light in her zealot's eyes. 'I'm related to the family on my mother's side and my late husband was one of Tait's dearest friends.'

Late? Laura seized on that fatal word. 'So you're alone then,' she said, wondering if Philippa's sense of loneliness or bereavement had deranged her mind.

'I'm sure I don't need to discuss my affairs with you,' Philippa tugged on the long, lustrous strand of pearls around her throat. 'You think you're coming to some sort of Outback paradise, don't you, Miss Kenmore? It should be a revelation for you. I expect you know about Lorne and how he's making everyone's life a misery?'

'No I don't know, Mrs Hill.'

'He can have some simply terrifying moods and young James, though the family seem to adore him, can be perfectly hateful. I expect you'll be asked to look after James sometimes. The little governess couldn't take it any longer. Jessica tell you about that?'

'She did say his governess had just gone.'

'Covered with weals from where dear little Jamie had scratched her. Of course he denied it, little pet. Of course she fell in love with Tait in the usual crazy, wild manner. He can't seem to escape these appalling infatuations. Any female who stays on the property turns into a raging lunatic of love.'

'What about you?'

It was said so very squarely, Philippa blinked. 'My dear Miss Kenmore, I've only lately lost my husband.'

'I'm very sorry, but that still doesn't answer the question.'

'You are a reporter, aren't you?' Despite her brittle laugh Philippa seemed thrown off-balance. 'Let me try to explain something to you, Miss Kenmore. It will save all your disgusting delving. At one time Tait and I were very deeply in love but through a terrible misunderstanding nothing came of it. I had known my husband for years too and gradually I came to love him. I must have cried buckets since he's gone. It seems extraordinary but I miss him more now than when he was away from me when he was alive. He loved me passionately. Perhaps this is my misfortune. I inspire passionate love.'

'Really? I wouldn't be sorry about it,' Laura said.

'Afterwards,' Philippa said, not even hearing her, 'Tait offered comfort. He has such a tremendously strong shoulder to lean on.'

'Does this mean you've moved in?' Laura asked very blandly.

'It means, Miss Kenmore,' Philippa returned acidly, 'I stay at Eagle's Ridge for as long as I like. Jessica has always loved to have me. This is truly the first occasion she hasn't followed my judgment. Thank heavens I'll be around to see how you're going to behave.' Philippa laughed with a frightful little helplessness. 'Please, please, don't waste your time falling in love with Tait.'

'I promise I won't pay him any attention.'

'You're very good at being flippant,' Philippa observed bitingly, 'but I'm sure you will—like all the rest. And you've shown us you haven't got a high moral sense. Tait likes a pretty face as much as the next man—maybe more. He's very susceptible to beauty, it's a family trait—but he wouldn't consider marrying outside his own circle. I'm sure you appreciate that?'

'It certainly saves looking further,' Laura said. 'And it's kept him single all these years. Now you really must excuse me, Mrs Hill, I left the Rolls in a loading zone.'

'That will never be,' Philippa returned tartly, anxious to have the last word. 'You should stay at home with your own kind.'

It was a worse scene when Laura called back at the office. Tucker was white and shaking, the very picture of a man who had been pinned to the wall.

'I always knew you were the rotten apple,

Kenmore,' he accused her. 'All women are trouble. Thanks for telling McEwan!'

'You'd rather we tell all about him?'

'That's our job!' Tucker yelled, almost dancing with rage. 'Now collect your things and clear out. You're dead in this business. By the time I'm finished there won't be a person to help you. Think about that while you're stuck in the sticks.'

'It was marvellous, marvellous!' Marty later told her with relish. 'To see someone reduce Tucker to a little frightened man!'

'I suppose he had to,' Laura said.

'God, girl, do you think anyone else but Tucker would have sacked you for sticking to your principles?'

'What about Max Gould?'

Marty considered it, crumpling a sheet of typing paper and throwing it into the waste-paper basket. 'All right, so Gould might have sacked you too. They're decent people over at *Metropolitan*, though. A few months will pass. I'm sure you'll have a good time—learn a lot. I'd like to be passing the time of day with a bunch of millionaires. You could even charm Sutton into giving you an exclusive some time. All legit. of course. Listen,' Marty leaned a little nearer her, hissing in her ear. 'You might even be able to land the cattle baron. Now there's one terrific looking guy! Sorry if this sounds crude, but he looks as sexy as hell. I'll bet there are throngs of women stumbling over their shoes trying to angle an invitation.'

'He only proposes to his own kind,' Laura was packing up swiftly as she spoke.

'Hey?' Marty's humorous eyes lightened and widened.

'I have it on authority that he only romances his own sort.'

'Oh, how splendidly snobby!' Marty crowed. 'He doesn't look that kind of guy to me. He looks a real person. Write to me and tell me how you're getting on.'

Tucker, still white-faced and sweating barged out of his door, putting an end to their chatter. 'See you, Marty,' Laura said as airily as she could when she was really very upset.

'You bet you will, darlin'', Marty said. 'Do you think we were just going to let you go? All of us want to take you out to dinner. I'll give you a ring.'

'All right, Collins,' Tucker yelled, 'so you want to hang on to your job?'

'I sure do.' Marty turned to confront the bulging, charging figure. 'I was hoping to see you later to discuss a little raise.'

At the door Laura lifted her hand and gave the general office a little wave. All responded with a look of deep mutiny on their faces. Tucker saw it too and returned to his office like a general suddenly unsure of his troops. One thing he was certain of, if he had to give Collins a raise, he was determined on putting paid to Kenmore's career. She had gone straight over to the enemy. McEwan's visit had left a horrible taste in his mouth. He badly needed a drink.

CHAPTER FOUR

JUST over a week later, Laura was on a commercial flight heading for the south-west of the great state of Queensland. On and off, ever since the Prince and Princess of Wales' historic visit of 1983, the great Outback, perennially in the grip of drought, had experienced heavy and prolonged flooding and now that the flood waters were finally receding the limitless barren plains looked more like luxuriant jungles. The desert earth was covered in lush grasses and bushes, sweet, cattle-fattening herbage and wild flowers in every conceivable colour from delicate to brilliant covered vast open tracts, shimmering to the horizon so the aerial view was fantastic.

'It's always like this,' a laconic old westerner told Laura confidingly. 'Either a feast or a famine. Hell or the Promised Land. If we're not carrying the fattest cattle on earth, we're losing them in the drought. It all goes in cycles. I have the feeling the good years have come back.'

That seemed to be the general feeling. Despite the hardship and isolation of severe flooding when the entire Outback seemed to be underwater and many recalled the inland sea of prehistory, nothing could be counted against the enormous benefits of an Inland revitalised. Trouble-worn graziers and stockmen skipped in the streets. The Outback was flourishing and every river, every creek, every waterhole was carrying clear water. It was incongruously marvellous, the semi-arid plains abundant in vegetation, the blood-red sandhills veined with great trails of white and gold everlastings. Laura found it so moving her heart rose to her throat. This landscape was more poignant than the lush beauty of the seaboards and immeasurably more powerful. This was the essence of the great island continent, the vast interior with its masterful strength. It must have appeared like another planet to the great explorers, men of tremendous courage and endurance who had come for the most part from the misty, jewelled settings of the British Isles. They could never have encountered such immensity before or the terrifying splendour of the great deserts that covered almost half the continent Supermen, Laura thought. A special breed the rest of us owe a great debt to. First the explorers . . . next the pioneers. She understood now what set men like McEwan apart. They drew their power from the landscape and it was certainly a marvellous thing to inherit a vast cattle kingdom. She had tried, ineffectually, to put him out of her mind but this had only served to increase his memorability. She would have to pray now.

By the time Laura reached the major Outback town where she was to wait until someone from Eagle's Ridge came for her, she was feeling very travel weary indeed. She had been many hours in the air and now she was the least little bit giddy. Perhaps it had something to do with her inner ear? At any rate, she couldn't do anything but try to walk a straight line. A bright sun was blazing and she could feel her hair start to cling to her scalp. A cold shower would be a great blessing!

She had been sitting in the terminal less than thirty minutes when an official came over to tell her eagerly that Mr McEwan had just landed.

'Are you sure it isn't someone else from the station?' Laura couldn't see that she rated the great man himself.

'Oh no, Miss. No one else flies Mr McEwan's personal plane.'

'Then you'd better go and roll out the red carpet.'

'Indeed we will,' the man smiled at her, seeing her expression was humorous. 'The McEwans are royalty in this part of the world.'

When he was gone Laura tipped her head back and shut her eyes. She feared her condition was worsening. What was it, vertigo? Certainly the long hours of flying time had brought it on. A young woman attendant had very kindly brought her a couple of aspirin but unfortunately they hadn't done the trick. She really needed to lie down.

'Are you all right?' A well-remembered voice asked her very crisply.

'Oh—I'm sorry.' Her eyes flew open in a flash and she tried to stand up. One couldn't sit with royalty, or was she supposed to kneel?

'What the devil——' He caught her arm.

'I'm a little dizzy. It will go away in a moment or two.'

He was silent for a moment, staring down at her. She had only seen him dressed very elegantly in his city clothes, now he was the cattle baron; twin-pocketed bush shirt in a bleached shade of blue, tight jeans that showed off his narrow waist, lean hips and long legs, high polished boots and because she was staring downwards she particularly noticed the silver buckle of his belt. It would have done credit to one of those characters out of Dallas. He looked terrific and about seven feet tall.

'Laura?' He sounded anxious and exasperated.

'That's some belt. Where did you find it?'

'I'll buy you one just like it if you like. Look, it's obvious there's something wrong with you. What is it?'

She lifted her head and her smoke-coloured eyes focused on his face. 'I can't really diagnose it. Vertigo perhaps. I had no idea how long it took to get to you.'

'Have you had these attacks before?' He pressed her back on to the upholstered bench.

'A few years ago when I flew to Auckland. Never fear, I'll recover.'

'When?' Frowning he looked violently, exotically handsome. 'Today, tomorrow, a week from now? Do you feel ill?'

'Vaguely nauseated.'

'How bloody awful!'

'You mean you want to sack me?'

'Just stop talking,' he told her. 'I'll arrange to get us to the hotel. It's obvious you're not flying anywhere else today.'

'You're very good to me, Mr McEwan,' she murmured, feeling increasingly peculiar. 'I haven't even thanked you for coming for me.'

'I said—shut up.'

'I expect the next will be a blow.'

She heard his tongue click against his teeth in irritation, then the young woman attendant was sitting with her.

'Mr McEwan has gone to get a car.'

'How marvellous! I don't think I could walk.'

'You really have gone a funny colour,' the girl told her. 'I expect it was all that travelling. Some people find it the end!'

The girl continued to talk to her, but Laura wished she would stop. Of course she meant well but somehow the talk was making her head swim.

'All right, Laura,' McEwan was back again. 'I'll take you out to the car.'

'I'm really sorry about this,' she said almost crossly but as she went to stand up with McEwan's assistance she knew at once she wouldn't make it. 'Oh God!' the tears of helplessness swam into her eyes.

'Is it possible you can bring those few things out to the car?' McEwan asked the girl attendant very briskly, going through the motions with no expectation of a refusal. She blushed and nodded but he had already turned away, scooping Laura up and carrying her like a feather weight out to the waiting station wagon.

He even had a doctor lined up at the hotel who gave Laura an injection and advised a good sleep. It wasn't unusual he told her for airplane travellers to suffer such disturbances. She would probably be as

good as new in the morning, when new wasn't all
that good.

It was an unheard of thing to keep McEwan waiting
but even then Laura never expected to hear him say
the thing he did: 'I suppose it's another of your little
plots?'

'I beg your pardon?' She tried to come away from
the pillows but he pressed her back.

'It doesn't matter. I'll rather like sitting here
watching you sleep.'

'No thank you!' The very idea was acutely
disturbing.

'How else am I going to occupy my time?' His
mocking expression became faintly sensual, his eyes
touching on the line of her body.

'I'm sure everyone in this town expects "Mr
McEwan" to behave properly,' she murmured, not
quite distinctly. 'What was in that injection, do you
suppose?'

When Laura opened her eyes again briefly it was to a
blood-red sunset. A fan was whirling in her room,
sending out sweet draughts of cooling air. She had
taken off her dress and was wearing her slip but even
then the light coverlet was too much for her. She
blinked and frowned up at the ceiling a few times but
her eyelids were incredibly heavy. The brilliant rosy
light was invading the room, colouring the long gauzy
curtains at the French windows, glinting from the
glass panes. How beautiful it was, like a dream.

When she awoke again it was to positive stillness
and a great fright. With horror she saw there was
someone—something—at the door. She had to get
away from it. She let out an agonised shriek and at this
point became entangled in the top sheet and the thin,
lemon coverlet, clawing wildly while her drugged
brain began to become illuminated by returning sense.
It was the curtain, of course. Moving on the night
breeze. She was in a strange, Outback hotel room,

McEwan was next door and she was safe. She moaned aloud in sheer relief. Her heart was still pounding in agitation and the sound of her strangled scream hung in the air. She ducked her head and took a deep breath, praying no one had heard her.

Suddenly with no warning the room was bathed in brilliant light. McEwan was standing in the connecting doorway looking so coiled and dangerous Laura very nearly screamed again. His eyes raced around the room then he moved very swiftly to the French windows, stepping out on to the verandah.

'For God's sweet sake can't you lie down properly?'

Freed from the belief he had startled an intruder his anxiety had turned to anger. 'I thought at the very least someone was trying to rape you.'

'That would please you wouldn't it?' she cried a little wildly, still suffering from shock.

'I'm sorry, Laura,' he said abruptly. 'I'd have killed him.'

'Damn it.' The sheet was wound around her like an Egyptian mummy.

'Here——'

'Don't touch me,' she said emotionally, 'Please.'

'OK, so get yourself out of it.'

'Wretched thing.'

He grew tired of watching her struggle so he leaned over and stripped the sheet away. 'If I had any idea you were going to be such a bloody nuisance——'

'You don't understand physical weakness, do you?'

'Let's just be quiet for a moment,' he said. 'I guess we both had a fright.' He sat down on one side of the bed while Laura wound her arms around herself on the other. Now all of a sudden she was very conscious of how little she wore, though her slip covered her as adequately as many a flimsy evening dress.

'Can't you turn off that damned light?' she asked crossly.

'Do you just want us to sit here in the dark?'

'No.'

'Neither do I.' He laughed.

'This is a laughing matter is it?' She threw her hair back and looked over her shoulder.

'Don't snap at me, sweet one,' he mocked her. 'How do you feel now?'

'Hungry, if you must know.'

He laughed again very gently in his throat. 'I can make you a cup of tea or a cup of coffee. That's all.' He moved his arm to a switchboard on the wall, flicking on the bedside lights and turning off the overhead light.

'It was the curtain.' She forgot she was angry with him. 'I woke up very suddenly and I couldn't remember where I was. I dislike intruders, or even ghosts.'

'So it seems.' He held out his hand towards her. 'Get back into bed, Laura. I want to leave quite early in the morning.'

'You'd better go without me.'

'You know I won't.'

As soon as her fingers made contact with his, she began to tremble. She hadn't wanted to touch him in the first place.

'Come, come, you can think of me as a . . . brother.'

'I'm not thinking of you at all.' Indeed mind and body were shrinking from his presence. He was still in his jeans but his shirt hung open to the waist, his broad chest hard with muscle and dark with hair, concentrated masculinity that had Laura, for all her élan, a little frightened. His expression was amused, faintly mocking, but at the back of his eyes was a tight, deliberate control. 'I'm sorry I disturbed you,' she murmured, without looking at him.

Very slowly and carefully he pulled the sheet around her. 'You've no idea how vulnerable you look. All white and gold and half naked.'

'I am not!' Sensation stabbed at her like a rain of darts.

'Trust me, Miss Kenmore.' He leaned forward and

kissed her very gently and briefly on the mouth. 'Then
again, when I think how clever you are?'

She was staring at him, silver-gilt hair sliding down
her back, luminous eyes darkened, the deep V of her
pearl-coloured slip revealing the creamy swell of her
young breasts, all about her the aura of femininity and
fragility. 'If you mean I screamed deliberately?'

'You never know.' He curved a skein of her hair
around his finger.

'Just you get out of here!' She began to quiver,
feeling under the rush of anger a growing sexual
desire. Even the expression in his eyes seemed to
answer it, a peculiar chemistry neither of them could
do anything about.

'Remember who you're talking to, Miss Kenmore,'
he admonished her and drew the strap of her slip
firmer on to her shoulder. 'Now since I need my rest if
you don't, I'm going to go back to bed. I'm right
through that door if you need me. In fact, I think I'll
leave it open.'

'I'm perfectly all right now,' Laura said quietly.
'Please shut it.'

He turned to smile at her, jet-black hair tousled and
curling raffishly, green eyes gleaming in an expression
she was coming to know. 'I adore your modesty, but
I'll leave it ajar all the same. Hang it all, you could
disturb me again.'

Laura knew what she had to do. She slid down into
the narrow bed and turned away. Damn McEwan! All
her life she had never met another man like him.

Dawn was quickly upon them and Laura stretched out
in bed in outrage as he told her very crisply to 'rise
and shine'. She could appreciate he was used to rising
with the sun but she had been having the most
pleasurable dream. Actually McEwan was in it, to her
astonishment. They were dancing. Maybe her brain
waves had been damaged.

An early breakfast had been specially prepared for

them and served in the dining room. Almost a party, or a breakfast in the grand tradition. Laura was famished. In any case McEwan wasn't watching her too closely. He seemed a little withdrawn and preoccupied. Probably doubting · the wisdom of allowing her into his desert kingdom.

'How far away is it?' she asked as they were nearing the airstrip.

'No distance at all,' he returned firmly, 'so don't tell yourself you're going to be sick.'

'I never have that trouble,' she gritted her teeth. 'Having vertigo is a different thing to auto-suggestion.'

Fifteen minutes later they were airborne, a silken flight into the dense blue heavens, with the incredibly red earth flowing away to the distant horizons ... empty ... empty ... seemingly to infinity. It seemed to her tremendously glamorous to be able to fly one's own plane and even more staggering when it was a luxury executive one, but she didn't doubt McEwan merely thought of it as a work-horse. Her first sight of it at the airport had brought home forcibly to her that he was indeed a very rich man, but now sitting beside him she considered he wore his wealth easily, very relaxed about it, every-day.

'What's amusing you?' he asked.

'Nothing much.'

'Come on.'

Laura obeyed. 'I was thinking the rich are different. I mean just to accept private planes and sitting on a million acres. Not a thing you can't buy.'

'Except love and happiness and being able to escape tragedy.'

'Of course. But—well—I wasn't trying to be profound.'

'I expect you'd like to marry a millionaire?'

'I should have explained a millionaire has actually asked me,' Laura retorted tartly.

'What, did you go visiting him in the nursing home?'

'He wasn't an elderly man.'

'And you refused him?'

'I don't know why you should find that so extraordinary.' Laura turned her head and arched her fine brows at him. 'I couldn't marry anyone I didn't love.'

'I just hope he hasn't been keeping you all these years.'

'In a flat a man like you can't move in?' I'll show him, Laura thought. I won't venture another remark.

She need not have worried. He ignored her so it was no use to try and teach him a lesson. Besides, the Outback was such an amazing place she returned to asking him questions, veering right away from the personal and discussing the unique wilderness over which they were flying. The Channel Country was classified as a riverine desert, a complex lacework of interconnecting channel-like rivers and creeks. Only very recently it had formed a vast floodplain, its myriad watercourses fed by the northern monsoonal rains.

Eagle's Ridge, it seemed, withstood both drought and flood and as he spoke of it Laura saw the fierce love that was reflected in his eyes. He was intensely proud of his heritage. Dedicated to holding on to it. After a while Laura gave up asking questions and just sat back and listened. He made it all come alive, the land's moods and its secrets, the good seasons, bad seasons, white man, Aboriginal, the Dreamtime's strange gods.

She was certain she could write a fantastic article on McEwan—the man and his land. She couldn't remember being so intensely interested in another interviewee before and by now she had interviewed several international figures. It seemed to her they couldn't talk like McEwan, so she supposed the ability to express oneself so graphically ran in the family. She remembered how enchanted she had been with Jessica McEwan's first book, or the first Laura had read. It had opened up a new world to her; so rich and colourful and yes, downright bizarre. Not too many highly civilised people chose to live in splendid isolation with one of the great deserts of the world on their doorstep. Not many people could drive all day on their own land.

'Oh, we're losing altitude,' she commented. They had been cruising at 12,000 feet at a speed of 307 mph but within seconds Laura saw the altitude indicator move downwards.

'We're coming in over the station now.' They dropped further still then levelled out. 'As you can see, and you'll see even better now, the country is in marvellous condition. I suppose it's difficult for a city girl to appreciate what the rain has meant to us.'

'Oh, I don't think so.' She had turned her head staring downwards. 'One has only to see shots of dying cattle to know the suffering that exists. It must be tragic in the drought.'

'Killing,' he agreed bleakly. 'We're more fortunate than most at Eagle's Ridge. We have permanent water and plenty of bores and the plant life and animals have found different way of coping with the harsh environment, still it's desiccated to what you're looking at now.'

'It's magnificent—and awesome,' Laura said. She had never fully realised the great size of her own country until the last two days. Not only size, its tremendous emptiness. It was so strange to see unending wilderness areas and she supposed this might make Australia unique. It probably determined the special Australian character. Everyone had so much space to move around in, to experience the land unchanged in thousands of years. It was a timeless grandeur in a world where the precious natural landscapes were fast being wiped out. To Laura's fascinated eyes it was the most spectacular landscape she had ever seen; not the emerald green lushness of tropical Queensland or the gentler beauty of the

temperate zones and the chilly magnificence of
Tasmania, but an isolated remoteness quite distinct
from the rest of the continent. The colours and forms
were fantastic, the blood reds and rich browns, the
yellows, the ochres, the myriad bleached greens and
over and above it the extraordinary intensity of light,
with an uninterrupted sky of brilliant, metallic blue. It
would be too easy to get lost down there.

Several minutes later she could see the air strip
coming up and beyond that, dominated by an isolated
flat-topped mesa that glowed purple against the blue
sky was the great station's homestead and its wide
semicircle of satellite buildings.

'Oh, how splendid!' Laura burst out. 'I've never
seen anything remotely like it before.'

'You mean you haven't visited the stronghold of the
nation's cattle kings before. To a lot of people it's El
Dorado and our homesteads go by legendary names.'

It made Laura think she could write a vivid account
of all this until she had to forcibly remind herself that
she was here as a secretary. Just as she was thinking
this her gaze swept to McEwan and she found herself
flushing at his penetrating expression.

'Oh, and one other thing, Miss Kenmore,' he said
warningly, 'we've agreed you're at Eagle's Ridge as
my aunt's secretary.'

'I understand that perfectly.'

'You look to me like you're longing for a pad and
pencil.'

She looked into his green eyes and felt herself
melting, her flesh clamouring against all good sense.
Because he had kissed her, comforted her and held her
close, didn't mean he wouldn't cut her down instantly
if she attempted to hurt his family in any way. They
had been through mental and physical traumas and he
obviously considered it his job to protect them. He
looked desperately tough and determined no matter
how smoothly and elegantly that toughness was
glazed.

'What does it all mean?' he asked her with faintly amused eyes. 'The soft glances, the little gasp.'

'I was thinking you'd throw me to the lions if I upset the people you love.' Her voice was a little husky and the light seemed trapped in her beautiful, smoky eyes.

'Remember it,' he said gently, 'if you're planning some devil's work.'

Philippa had elected to meet them. Philippa and a little boy of five or six who hurtled towards Tait McEwan with an eager cry and a peal of laughter.

'Uncle Tait . . . Uncle Tait!'

In an instant McEwan caught him and hoisted him to shoulder level, on his strong, handsome face an expression Laura had never seen. It was tender, absorbed and it sent funny little tremors up and down Laura's spine. How this man might look at his son!

Philippa's cold eyes levelled over Laura and she greeted her tautly. 'How are you, Miss Kenmore, after your . . . indisposition?' Her tone was sharp and ironic, as though she believed it had been some kind of stratagem.

'Much better, thank you, Mrs Hill,' Laura looked back at her very blandly. 'We had a marvellous trip. Very quick and smooth.'

'Pray what else would it be with Tait?'

Tait McEwan was now kneeling down, talking to his small nephew who was showing him a grazed knee liberally doused with an orange-red paint. The child was a McEwan for all he was Lorne Sutton's son. Sweet and childish as it was now it was impossible not to detect the McEwan imprint on that satiny skinned little face.

Looking at them Laura could feel her face softening and McEwan stood up and with a charming smile introduced—Jamie.

'I'm sure you won't be allowed to call Miss

Kenmore, Laura,' Philippa said almost sternly when the little boy instantly used Laura's christian name.

'I don't see why not,' Tait McEwan intervened smoothly, 'I've been calling her Laura for some time.'

'May I call you Laura, please Laura?' the little boy asked and Laura found herself swallowing on a lump in her throat.

'I'd like that, Jamie,' she said, and all at once took his hand. 'I hope we're going to have lots of talks, and lots of walks. I think Eagle's Ridge is the most marvellous place on earth!'

Jamie laughed merrily, in the mysterious fashion of all creatures either liking or disliking another on sight. The fact his hand remained quite happily in Laura's was an unreserved mark of approval as was his insistence he would sit between his uncle and Laura.

McEwan settled it, touching the boy very lightly on the cheek. 'In the back, like a good boy. There are lots of things you can point out to Laura.'

In fact the first thing Laura exclaimed over brought forth more peals of laughter. She pointed to the most spectacular tree she had ever seen in her life. It rose about twelve feet off the ground, its totally bare limbs tortured beyond belief into the most fantastic shapes but what made it so extraordinary was its huge, glorious white flowers, like some never-before-seen species of magnolia.

'How extraordinary!' she cried out and as she did so Tait blew the horn of the station wagon and the whole tree exploded.

'Good heavens!'

'They're birds, Laura!' Jamie cried. 'Don't you know little corellas when you see them? The tree's dead.'

During the several minutes it took to arrive at the homestead there was plenty to exclaim over but Laura made no more mistakes. It was really like a small settlement she thought; the McEwans' private world. There were very many outbuildings, large and small and several neat bungalows set in their own gardens; a most unique community.

'Do you live in a big house, Laura?' Jamie asked. His tousled curls were the McEwan black and his wide, earnest gaze an exquisite greenish-blue.

'I live in a flat, Jamie,' she told him.

'What's that?'

'It's where you live when you're somewhat short of money,' Philippa supplied.

'We can lend you some, Laura,' Jamie mumbled so Philippa couldn't hear. 'Uncle Tait is the richest man in the world!'

If that wasn't quite true, Laura thought wryly, he certainly lived in a great pile of a house. It was magnificent, Colonial Georgian with wide, deep verandahs and two-storey columns, six in all, soaring to the great sweep of the roof. It could have been set down anywhere in some beautiful area of the British Isles or even, in particular, the American South. Instead it was overlooked and dominated by an ancient mesa that changed colour in different lights and at different times. Now from purple it had gone to an incredible pinky-crimson much as the jewels of the desert, the Olgas and Uluru-Ayers Rock, turned on their colour displays. Following her line of vision, Jamie told her excitedly that according to Aboriginal legend the mighty wedge-tailed eagle, Arrilka, mythical creature, had been born there.

'See, Laura, there's one of Arrilka's descendants now!' Jamie yelled and was immediately urged by Philippa to quieten.

Indeed a lone eagle was soaring high over the house, its powerful, outspread wings black against the sun.

'He lives up there,' Jamie whispered and pointed to the majestic mesa. 'We protect our eagles because they belong to Eagle's Ridge. An eagle like that could kill and carry off a sheep. They kill wallabies too. They're so powerful! Their wingspan is about seven feet, did you know?'

Jamie kept up his excited chatter until the station wagon came to rest at the base of a broad flight of steps up to the house. 'You won't be seeing Daddy today,' he confided and gestured towards the upper reaches of the house. 'Daddy hates people. New people, but I'm sure he won't hate you.'

'Don't fool yourself you've won Jamie over,' Philippa murmured to Laura as they were moving towards the front door. 'I fear he's as unpredictable as his father.'

CHAPTER FIVE

IT wasn't until late afternoon of the following day that Laura had her first glimpse of Lorne Sutton, the artist. She was reading very quietly in the library, completely hidden from the doorway by the enveloping wings of her leather armchair, when someone moved into the room behind her; a rather stealthy movement that surprised her. Jamie ran. The McEwans walked proudly, confidently, Philippa's footsteps positively rang, Mrs Lambert (Lamby as Jamie called her), the housekeeper, moved with calm deliberation and the two little Aboriginal housegirls Laura had seen pattered around like velvety brown mice. Therefore she half turned in her chair rather cautiously, seeing a medium-tall, very slim man avoid the eight-thousand volumes in the library and move to an antique cabinet that Laura soon saw housed a healthy collection of bottles of various sizes; fortified wines, liqueurs, spirits.

While Laura considered what she should do, the man very swiftly uncorked the Chivas Regal and poured himself a ruinously long drop. Then, without turning, he tossed it down all at once, his profile contorted as though he had just swallowed poison.

Good grief! Laura thought feebly and felt her own stomach shrink in protest. Perhaps she even made a tiny sound for the man wheeled on her in alarm, his coal-black eyes registering enormous shock, his olive skin turning grey. 'Who ... are *you*?' he almost whispered.

Instinctively Laura sought to reassure him. 'Forgive me for startling you. I was reading. I'm Laura Kenmore, Miss McEwan's new secretary.'

'New secretary?' Disbelief touched his face.

'I certainly am. I arrived yesterday, Mr Sutton.'
She was speaking very gently but freely, much as a
womanly woman would speak to a highly strung
young person. Except Lorne Sutton had to be at least
ten years older than herself.

'I see.' He looked shocked. 'Of course I was told,
but telling was not enough.'

'I'm sorry.' He seemed to find the sight of her so
intolerable Laura felt obliged to apologise for her
reality. 'I was just finished anyway, Mr Sutton, if you
wish to use the library.'

'No ... no.' He waved that suggestion away.
'You're Jessica's secretary. That's why you're here?'

'She can't type the book herself, Mr Sutton. I
understand Miss McEwan always writes her books in
beautiful longhand. One simply doesn't see handwrit-
ing like that any more.'

'No, indeed.' This unremarkable remark evidently
caught his low threshold of interest. 'You are writing a
book yourself?'

'I have had that ambition from time to time, but
writing books isn't all that easy to do. I very much
admire Miss McEwan.'

'That's good, that's good, she's a wonderful person,
a lovely, kind, human being.'

He wasn't, Laura saw, as good looking as his
photographs. They had always made him look
positively Byronic, but close to the dark intensity was
somehow muddied, or perhaps it wasn't a very strong
face. He was bone thin, not honed to the bone like
McEwan, a whole world of difference, but frail, not
fit. Nevertheless he compelled the eye for the
desperation that was in him, a desperation that
appeared to be eating him away.

'I'm looking forward to working for her,' Laura
murmured in sympathetic agreement. 'If you would
like to sit quietly here, Mr Sutton, I can go someplace
else.'

'I'm very tired. I can't sleep. Night after night.' He

raised his hand to his forehead and shrugged attractively. 'Please forgive me for my odd behaviour.'

Laura smiled with deep understanding in her eyes. 'Have you tried listening to music with a headset?' she asked him. 'I went through rather a bad period when it was the only thing that seemed to help.'

'You?' He stared at her for a few seconds as though trying to gauge her sincerity. 'You can't have had many bad moments. You're just a child.'

'Children know how to mourn.' She answered gently but deliberately. Didn't he know his own little boy was desperately missing his mother? Jamie's immediate attachment to her was proof he found comfort in a young and attractive woman. Of course he adored Aunt Jessica, but Aunt Jessica tired. Philippa was certainly young and good looking but she seemed to have no feeling for children. It was perhaps inevitable Jamie would take to another young person who liked him and speaking to him was easy. It was Nicky all over again trying to squeeze every minute out of the day. 'If you like,' she told him, 'I can lend you my little cassette recorder to see how you go. Many's the night I fell asleep to Mozart or Brahms or Vivaldi; piano concertos, violin solos, opera and ballet, anything and everything, except pop and military bands.'

Incredibly he laughed, a rusty sound as though he hadn't done it in a long time. 'And it really worked?'

'Nothing better,' she promised him. 'I would like you to try it. It's very difficult to manage without sleep. My father used to call it the "mending time". He was a doctor.'

'Was?' he asked quietly, his dark eyes seemingly trying to delve into her mind.

'My parents were killed four years ago,' Laura explained. 'It was a devastating blow.' She answered a little briskly as though she didn't want any painful memories opened up.

'How cruel life is,' he observed. 'A few rewards but mostly heartbreak.'

'I suppose we just have to be strong enough to absorb it. So many can make do on so little.'

'I've heard that before, my dear,' he said, very wearily. 'Some can handle grief. I simply don't know how.'

He left her abruptly and didn't appear again.

'What did you say to Daddy?' Jamie asked at tea-time.

'Why, darling?' They were sitting together in a corner of the huge kitchen where Jamie liked to have his evening meal.

'He had tears in his eyes.'

'Perhaps you were mistaken.' Laura felt a little shocked.

'I know what tears are like, Laura,' Jamie said and waved away more milk. 'I said, "What's wrong, Daddy?" and he said, "Clear off, Jamie, like a good chap". Most of the time he can't wait to get rid of me. I expect I remind him of Mummy.'

They were sitting at a bench seat and Laura put her arm around the child and hugged him to her. 'He loved her, Jamie. He loves you. He's recovering, you must give him time.'

'All right.' Jamie turned more fully towards her, lifting his glossy head. 'When do you suppose he's going to be better?'

'We must pray.' Laura very gently touched his face.

'Do you pray, Laura?'

'Yes I do.'

'So did Mummy, but prayers aren't part of Daddy's life.'

'Then I can see we'll have to do it for him. Now, what is that funny looking pudding? Is that yours?'

'Yes.' Jamie laughed. 'Lamby puts faces on all sorts of things. She used to draw them on my egg but I can eat them without these days.'

Mrs Lambert came to the table with a cup of coffee for Laura, her round character-filled face crinkling up in a smile. 'What about if I join the family?'

'Please.' Laura looked up to smile and Jamie pointed to where Mrs Lambert could sit.

'Love is a miracle,' Mrs Lambert said slowly. 'Love and warmth. I'm so happy, Miss Kenmore, that you and Jamie have taken to each other like a house on fire. You see, he has been a very lonely little boy.'

Tait McEwan didn't appear at dinner, but Laura and her employer chatted away happily, seemingly not minding that the third person at the table, Philippa, contrived to appear deliberately detached. Of course she answered when Jessica spoke to her, always in a painfully courteous way, but Laura, seeing how things were going, decided she would wait for Philippa to speak to her first. Philippa didn't.

'Poor unhappy girl!' Jessica said later. 'Something has really gone wrong with her since Jeff was killed. I think she's blaming herself for a number of things that are now far too late to mend. Be patient with her, Laura, if you can. Some people can cope—it's a sort of extra quality—and other's can't. I'm not young any more. All I can do is worry.'

'And write marvellous books.' Jessica pushed out the footstool so it was beneath Jessica's feet. 'Now, what are we going to do tomorrow? You've given me enough time to settle in.'

Jessica looked pleased. 'You're such a vital creature, aren't you, Laura? The moment I laid eyes on you I thought, now here's a girl who positively glows. And you're so good with Jamie. Philippa would tell you that is an art in itself. I'm afraid Jamie is rather in Philippa's bad books. He has let fly with her a few times. The McEwan temper which has to be curbed. In your case, however, he's another child again. Angelic!'

'So was Nicky, but it never lasted more than a few seconds.'

Jessica leaned over and patted Laura's hand. 'I expect you miss your Nicky terribly?'

'Yes I do. In the early days I used to think I'd go mad going home to the empty house. I used to look around for him all the time but then the letters came and he sounded so happy. I wanted to howl.' Laura gave the older woman a starry smile. 'I was missing him more than he was missing me, he was always occupied with the other boys and games. He's amazingly good at sports. Anyway, he loves it.'

'Why don't you invite him out here for the Easter holidays?' Jessica suggested. 'You don't have to find any money. He comes as our guest.'

'Why, Miss McEwan!'

'You're surprised?'

'I'm delighted.' Laura flushed. 'You're too good.'

'I'm curious about this young brother,' Miss McEwan said. 'I want to look at him. See if he's as handsome as his sister is beautiful.'

'He's very like me,' Laura said. 'You don't want to think any more about this, Miss McEwan?'

'Actually it was Tait who said the boy should pay us a visit. No, write to him, my dear and let him know. I expect a boy his age would be thrilled at the very idea.'

'Indeed he will.' Laura felt elated herself. To have Nicky here would be marvellous. Something she never dreamed of. It had been organised he would stay with Uncle Clive, now perhaps she could angle an extra day for him.

'And by the way,' Miss McEwan said, studying Laura's suddenly radiant face, 'I think you had best call me Jessica, or Aunt Jessica, if you like as Philippa does. "Miss McEwan" sounds terribly aloof.'

Tait McEwan came in about nine o'clock, looking somewhat grim. Laura watched him walk towards them, thinking he was a man of many expressions. This one was distinctly formidable.

'Darling, you look upset.'

'It's taken time to unravel who was responsible for Charlie's running off.'

'I suppose he was afraid,' Jessica McEwan said simply.

'Aren't they all when they break the rules? But they will do it. I think it's come down to Charlie has taken a fancy to Jacky's promised bride.'

'Jacky's grandfather is a celebrated sorcerer in these parts,' Jessica explained for Laura's wide-eyed benefit. 'A young buck would take a terrible risk crossing Mindji or any member of his family. Without doubt he'd make some special bad magic.'

'I'll have to round up the old devil in the morning,' Tait said shortly, though his eyes held a hint of humour. 'Charlie is too valuable to me. He probably shouldn't be looking at Lily but you can bet your life Lily has been making plenty love magic of her own. I'm sure I prefer Charlie to Jacky.'

'You must want your dinner,' Jessica said. 'You mustn't work so hard.'

'I can't find anyone else to do it for me,' Tait said. 'You two look very comfortable together.'

'I believe we took to one another at first sight,' Jessica said comfortably. 'Do you think you could tell Mrs Lambert Tait is in, Laura? I'm for an early night if nobody minds.'

Tait shot his aunt a very penetrating look at the same time assisting her to her feet. 'If you are feeling the least little bit unwell you must tell me.'

'Darling, I'm fine. Fine.' She lifted her head to his lowered one and kissed his cheek. 'But a girl does need her beauty sleep.'

'You're not hiding anything, Jessie?'

'You spoke to Dr Adams, darling,' his aunt reminded him. 'You're doing a very good job of looking after your aunt.'

The underlying bleak importance of this conversation visibly upset Laura. She looked from one to the other and Aunt Jessica explained quietly. 'I have a little heart condition, Laura. Nothing all that serious, so don't you worry. I'm sure I don't. So long as I follow my doctor's orders all will be well. And if you're now wondering why we're going to work on my book it's because I so enjoy it. Besides, we've only got to get it together, you and I. With your training you're going to be a very big help.'

'Tait?' Laura asked gravely after Aunt Jessica had gone. 'It's not serious, is it?'

He ran a bronzed hand through his night-wind rumpled hair. Like Jamie's it was inclined to curl in profusion. 'Adams told me with care she has a lot more years in her. Those were his very words. She insists on finishing this book. Her best, she says. And she does enjoy it. Whatever you were up to, Laura, I know you're now going to be a big help to her.'

'Will you ever let me live it down?' She flushed and threw him a quick look.

'I've got a lot of worries at the moment,' he told her implacably, 'it wouldn't be safe to add to them.'

'I'll go and speak to Mrs Lambert,' she murmured and swung about.

'Maybe you can look after me,' he said.

'Are you sure you trust me?' she asked ironically.

'Certainly you can take a meal out of the oven?'

Every minute she was with him Laura had the same feeling of racing in top gear. 'Come into my kitchen, said the spider to the fly.'

'I'll go along with that.'

The kitchen was a wonderful room. Almost as big as Laura's former flat. One entire end wall was composed of floor-to-ceiling louvres that opened on to a magnificent, cool fernery and provided flow-through ventilation for the large room. Everything was natural; slate, brick and beautiful gleaming woods in the homestead tradition, but it was ultra modern when it came to the aids and nearly all of them on the commercial restaurant scale. At different times during the year it was almost open-house on the station when crowds of visitors—relatives, friends, business associates came to stay—and Mrs Lambert found she really needed her handsome, appliance-filled domain.

Laura found herself some padded gloves and opened the door of the wall oven. 'It looks very much like Mrs Lambert has left you this.'

'She knew I would be coming in late,' Tait confirmed. He turned away to look at the dining alcove, finding it as usual when he was late neatly set. 'Are you going to join me?'

'You're joking!' Laura exclaimed faintly. 'I've had a marvellous dinner. I shan't be able to keep it up.'

'Because of that gorgeous figure?'

'Yes,' she agreed seriously. 'Most people watch their diet these days, you know.'

'I don't.' He made a faintly weary gesture.

'I expect you'd burn a million calories off.' Laura set the casserole dish down, lifting the glass lid. 'Hmm, delicious! I'd say it was Boeuf Bourguignon.'

'I still want it.' He seemed amused by the sight of her. 'Has Jamie worn you out?'

'Not at all, we're good friends. Oh, there's rice too by the look of it.'

'Hurry, Laura, hurry,' he said and waited as calmly as Jamie for everything to be brought to him. Whatever violent exertions he managed outdoors he had no thought to attend to his own meals. There were women to do that.

What else is a good woman for? Laura thought humorously.

'Don't go,' he said when she looked like running off.

'I thought you might want to eat in peace.'

'You're mad. There's a great deal to be said for a beautiful woman across the table.'

'Oh well, if I cheer you up.' She smiled at him and slid on to the comfortably upholstered seat. 'I wonder if you could do something for me?'

'I can't.' He was forking into the rich casserole with evident enjoyment.

'Please.'

'If you want a good night kiss, Laura, just carry on

the way you are.' He looked up very quickly, his green cat's eyes gleaming maliciously.

'No kisses, thank you,' she said. 'I was speaking to Mr Sutton late this afternoon . . .'

'You were what?'

'Why . . . you heard me,' she floundered.

'What are you, Laura, some kind of a witch?' He gave her face, her hair, her shoulders a quick, all-over glance. 'I was certain Lorne had gone into hiding for at least a week.'

'He was in the library.'

'Aah!' He returned to his meal briskly.

'I don't know what "aah" means . . .'

'Oh?' One winged black eyebrow shot up. 'Did you think it rather hard?'

'Mr Sutton confided he has great difficulty sleeping at night.'

'Do please be careful, Laura,' he told her, a curious expression on his dark, handsome face.

'I recognise insomnia when I see it. I suggested he might like to try my little Walkman.'

'What?'

'Of course it's only a suggestion.'

'What the hell is your little Walkman?'

'What indeed!' She eyed him coolly. 'It's one of those little cassette recorders. You know with a headset. I found it invaluable for soothing me off to sleep.'

'I expect a husband might do that in time.'

'Would you please give it to Mr Sutton?' she pleaded. 'It's worth a try.'

'I think I'm obliged to have a drink.' Abruptly he stood up, walked to the huge, walk-in pantry and came back with a bottle of red wine.

'I know where the opener is,' Laura said helpfully, but when she went to push up he urged her by exerting a little pressure to remain seated.

'And what else did you suggest to Lorne?' He returned to the table with the wine and two tulip-shaped glasses.

'We barely exchanged a few words.'

'Yet, as you say, he confided.'

'Was it a mistake to talk to him?' She was reacting to his tone.

'You have so many talents, Laura. All there for us to see. And hidden.'

'For God's sake, what's wrong with trying to help someone?' she cried.

'Settle down, smoky-eyes.'

'You sound angry, disturbed. I don't understand.' Agitation made her put out a hand to him.

'What wonderful skin you've got, Laura.' He glanced at her creamy fingers against the bronzed skin of his arm. 'I should think it would be perfect to paint.'

'Paint?' Now it was her turn to looked surprised.

'Any man who didn't think you beautiful would be a perfect fool,' he returned, quite curtly.

'Hold on,' she said laconically, 'I'm missing some part of this.'

'From what I've seen of you, Laura, you don't miss a thing.'

From ease there was almost an antagonism between them, so eventually she said: 'I assure you my motives are most unselfish. I can't bear to see anyone suffer if I can help.'

He sipped his wine, saying nothing, just looking at her. For coolness she had arranged her hair on top of her head with several silken floating strands and the lovely fluid line of her arched neck made her look like a top-heavy flower on a graceful stem. Her thin dress in the palest shade of pink completed the picture.

'And you require me to take this recorder along to Lorne?'

'If you'd be so kind.' Her deeply moulded mouth curled a shade derisively.

'Ouch!' she gasped and sat back.

'Don't adopt that tone with me.' With a swift

motion he rubbed the little red mark on her arm. 'God, you'd bruise easily.'

'Most people don't pinch me.'

'Then you've never been to Italy.'

'Would you take it to Mr Sutton?' she asked.

'All right,' he agreed quietly. 'Do you like the wine?'

'It's wonderful!'

'Among other things I own a vineyard in South Australia. We seem to be doing better all the time. A German family run it for me. Migrated about ten years ago. Marvellous people, perfectionists. It's in the blood.'

Laura lifted her wineglass up to the light, circling the ruby liquid around. 'I want to thank you for suggesting Nicky might come out here.'

'You'll want to see him.' It wasn't a question but a plain statement.

'You can't know how much. Nicky is all I have left.'

'Of course.' His expression was unexpectedly gentle. 'But you'll have children of your own one day.'

'I hope so.' She nodded. 'I would very much want them.'

'And what about a husband, little one? Do you want him too?'

'A husband, first. Next, the children.' She took another sip of the jewelled wine.

'Have you ever been in love?'

'Have you?'

'Passingly.' He set down his glass and smiled, a devastating white flash in his darkly tanned face. 'How many men have been in love with you, silly Laura? Apart from the elderly millionaire?'

'Let's see.' Her luminous eyes unfocused, staring into the past. 'There was a boy called Robert in the Fourth Grade. He loved me because I used to get my sums all wrong.'

'No one now?' he asked with a surprisingly direct look.

'No.' She blinked. 'What is this, Mr McEwan, the third degree?'

'I don't want any surprises when I find out.'

Neither of them heard the approaching footsteps until they were at the door.

'That's probably Mrs Lambert,' Tait said casually. 'We'll have to tell her you've done her job.'

Laura wished it might have been Mrs Lambert, but a very different woman swept across the room. a dozen emotions chasing across her pale face as her eyes took in the companionable scene. She had discarded the clothes she wore at dinner for an exquisite Wedgwood-blue satin nightgown and matching peignoir. Laura had never seen such beautiful nightwear in her life. For that matter, where did one buy it? Only Linda Evans or Joan Collins had that kind of gear.

'Oh,' she faltered, and her jagged breath came painfully. 'I wanted to talk to you, Tait.'

Laura was already standing. 'I'll say good night. If it's not any trouble, Mr McEwan, I'll leave the recorder and a few cassettes on the circular library table.'

'Thank you, Miss Kenmore.' He lifted his glass and saluted her. 'Your wish shall be obeyed.'

'What wish?' Philippa demanded, her delicate nostrils dilated.

'Just a little idea that might help Lorne sleep,' Tait told her. 'She's very clever, our Miss Kenmore.'

'Too clever, don't you think?' There was an icy sneer in Philippa's voice.

'She's had to work at it,' Tait murmured humorously. 'She told me in the Fourth Grade she was no good at her sums.'

It was nonsense, of course, but as Laura glanced back she saw Philippa slide quickly into the dining alcove. Not opposite Tait as Laura had been, but close up beside him, so he had to be reeling under the impact of the sumptuous peignoir that showed the taut nipples of her slight breasts and the heady draught of

her perfume, a complex floral bouquet with head notes
of gardenia.

Laura wondered, yet again, how long Philippa had
known him and whatever had gone wrong in their ill-
starred past. Surely he must still care about her, for
how else would she be here at Eagle's Ridge? As much
as Laura was attracted to Tait McEwan, she
recognised her knowledge of him was slight. Also deep
inside her something was protesting at the very idea of
their ... involvement. After all she *was* a fairly recent
widow; the late husband had been a very close friend.
Life was full of the most extraordinary, impossible
things. Philippa, the old girlfriend making a comeback.
Perhaps he was too kind to simply throw her out? He
had demonstrated even in her own case he was quite a
caring person.

And so it went on. Laura argued with herself for a
full half hour before she shut her eyes. The best thing
she could possibly do was not follow her own
dangerous inclinations. Men like Tait McEwan could
be counted on for inspiring a desperate infatuation. It
would be hard enough to deal with the look of him,
the sound of him, without Eagle's Ridge thrown in.
She was even filled with an exasperated pity for
Philippa. She had loved him for a long time. He
wouldn't have had to try very hard to become her
lover, next family friend. Maybe it was only in fairy
stories that people lived happily ever after.

Laura eventually went off to sleep feeling truly
disturbed about Tait McEwan. She didn't need or
want a major complication in her life and he was well
and truly a complication. Even touching the tips of his
fingers was like touching a live wire. Allowing her
fascination to grow would be the same as exposing
herself to grave danger.

CHAPTER SIX

THE next morning something totally unexpected happened. Lorne Sutton made an appearance at the breakfast table.

'A morning to remember!' Mrs Lambert hissed as Laura, on Tait's instructions, hurried into the kitchen to tell her. 'Thank you, dear. And where is Master Jamie?'

'He's come down with me.' Laura didn't add Jamie had woken her up at six o'clock with a request to help him put together the 3-stage space command ship with two cockpits, a space lab and landing pad she had brought him as a present.

Mrs Lambert laughed, looking at Laura with pleasure and approval. 'You seem to be Jamie's guardian angel. You even look like one with that beautiful shining hair down your back.'

When she returned to the beautiful breakfast room set aglow by a huge, arched stained glass window and a collection of English porcelain plates decorating the walls, Tait was speaking quietly to his brother-in-law, who stood up immediately and held the seat beside him for Laura.

'Good morning, Mr Sutton,' she smiled at him. 'Did you find Signor Vivaldi a help?'

'Salvation.' He gave a funny little moan and closed his eyes for a moment.

'You can take it, Miss Kenmore,' Tait said briskly 'your suggestion did a power of good. I'm rather disgusted I didn't think of it myself.' In the morning light he looked vividly, brilliantly alive and she was suddenly shaken by the most appalling desire to touch him. 'What is it?' he asked abruptly and frowned.

'I wanted you to sit beside me, Laura,' Jamie saved

her from having to find an answer by raising his
voice rather querulously. One would have thought
he would be agreeably surprised to find his father at
the table, instead his handsome little face almost
looked jealous.

'What do you mean sit beside Laura?' Tait
demanded. 'I'm here. If you're going to sit beside
anyone come and sit beside your uncle.'

'I can't sit in that chair.'

'Yes, you can.'

'Oh beaut!' Jamie scrambled to sit on one of the
magnificent high-backed Gothic chairs, instead of the
cushioned armchair Mrs Lambert had brought into
the room for his use. 'I guess this means I'm all grown
up?'

'Almost,' his uncle smiled. 'You might bring one of
those cushions and it will give you a bit of extra
height.'

'Porridge, Laura,' Jamie said, clutching a cushion to
his chest. 'Lamby said I must have it.'

'My God!' Lorne Sutton looked as though the
thought of a bowl of porridge filled him with horror.

'The beneficial effect of porridge in the morning is
proven,' Tait said lightly. 'Indeed without your
porridge you'll never grow to be as tall as I am.'

'Then I'll have it right away.'

'What could be more natural for someone called
Jamie McEwan,' Laura smiled.

'You're getting mixed up, Laura,' Jamie told her.
'I'm James Andrew Sutton. I'm a McEwan on
Mummy's side.'

'Of course you are, chicken,' Laura looked up and
flushed a little. 'That was a silly thing to say. I wasn't
thinking—except how like your uncle you are.'

'Is that why you like me, Laura?' Jamie went on,
looking from his uncle to Laura as though this was an
interesting point.

'You must know I like you for yourself.'

'Couldn't we try the porridge?' Tait intervened

smoothly. 'Laura can't very well say she doesn't like me, after all.'

Laura rose to attend to the child and Jamie cried eagerly. 'Did you see the wonderful Lego Laura brought me, Uncle Tait? We've been working all morning to try and put it together.'

'You mean you've been disturbing, Miss Kenmore?' his father removed his hand from his temple and stared across at Jamie with stern eyes.

'Not at all!' Laura rushed to protest.

'We had a wonderful time.' Jamie suddenly threw a tantrum.

'Don't shout at me, young man,' Lorne Sutton said intensely. 'I'm not at all happy about your rude, uncontrolled behaviour. If you're going to shout, in future you won't be allowed to come to the table.'

'I will too!' Jamie glared at his father with odd hostility. 'Uncle Tait is the boss here, you know.'

'Yes,' Tait McEwan sat back rather grimly, 'and since you are being, Jamie, extremely rude, you can apologise to your father this minute.'

Jamie muttered something violent beneath his breath and at the same time Lorne Sutton dragged back his chair explosively. 'I don't understand what this child is becoming.'

'This is one of those times you're noticing, Lorne,' Tait McEwan told him bluntly. 'You've ignored him for months.'

'Get up, Jamie,' Laura said swiftly and in a voice that brooked no defiance. 'We'll have breakfast in the kitchen.'

'Don't go on my account, Miss Kenmore,' Lorne Sutton said stiffly. 'I really only came to the table to thank you for your understanding and your kindness.'

'Well please stay, Mr Sutton,' Laura answered quickly, taking hold of Jamie's shoulders. 'I'm sure when Jamie settles down he'll come to you and tell you he's sorry he was rude.' In truth she felt a little uncomfortable under Lorne Sutton's beseeching stare.

He had been a little grim with the child and lonely little Jamie had reacted.

'Might I be excused, Miss Kenmore?' Tait McEwan asked in a heavily mocking voice.

'I'm sorry, Uncle Tait,' Jamie suddenly cried, his rosy face crumpling. 'I won't bother you, Daddy.'

It was the moment for Lorne Sutton to catch his little son up, instead he turned away his face very pale. 'The sooner we find a good boarding school for you, the better,' he pronounced, then stalked away.

Laura, standing holding Jamie, felt she couldn't believe her ears. 'Boarding school?' she eyed Tait McEwan incredulously. 'He's only five years old!'

'I won't go!' Jamie sobbed, turning his wet face into Laura's skirt and thumping her on the hip. 'I won't leave here. Not ever!'

'Come on now, Jamie.' Tait McEwan did what the child's father should have done. He scooped up the boy, holding the child at face level. 'Stop all that moaning and muttering. Do you know what being grown up means? It means you must respect yourself and other people. No matter how you feel, you cannot shout at your father. You must explain quietly, if you can.'

'He hates me,' Jamie gulped, tears streaming down his face.

'He does not.'

'Yes he does,' Jamie sighed. 'I don't want to go to boarding school, Uncle Tait.'

'There's no boarding school, Jamie. Not for quite a time. Years.'

'Truly?' Suddenly Jamie brightened up.

'Yes,' Tait replied quietly. 'When you upset your father, he retaliates. It's not the time now, but later on today I want you to go to him and tell him you're sorry about this morning. You are, aren't you?'

'Whenever I go to speak to him he tells me to go away,' said Jamie. 'He doesn't need me to speak to. Maybe it's my face that makes him angry.'

'Your face? Why would you think that?' his uncle asked him.

Jamie broke down again. ''Cause I remind him of . . . of . . . Mummy,' he whispered.

'God Almighty!' Tait McEwan looked directly into Laura's distressed eyes. 'How could he be allowed to think that?'

'He's been trying to find the answer himself,' she said haltingly. 'He's such a little boy.' She reached out and instinctively began patting Jamie's back. 'He is like his mother?' she asked softly.

'As a matter of fact,' Tait said angrily, 'he takes after me. Anne was more the Seymour side of the family. We shared the same colouring and a certain family look, but Jamie doesn't really have his mother's features. He's like his grandfather. You've seen the portrait of him when he was young—the boy in the library.'

'I thought it was you!'

'Of course it's not me,' Tait said testily, 'it's my father. He was painted with his favourite horse.'

'I want a horse too,' Jamie said. 'Daddy only gets angry with me because I can't draw.'

'My darling heart, what's happened?' Mrs Lambert asked when Jamie, tears dripping and holding Laura's hand, went back into the kitchen.

'Nothing much,' Laura headed Mrs Lambert off quietly. 'We haven't had our breakfast as yet. I'm afraid Jamie's porridge will be cold.'

'So I'll make some more.' Mrs Lambert's pity-filled eyes moved swiftly to Laura. 'I thought I heard raised voices.' She had, in fact, been attempting to listen at the door.

'No one planned it that way. Come and sit down, Jamie,' Laura said. 'I want to talk to you about boarding school later on. Much later on as your uncle said, and it's not a bad place. My brother, Nicholas, goes to boarding school. He loves it.'

'Does he really?' Jamie moved quickly to slip into the alcove. 'I thought it was a terrible place to stay.'

'Not at all. Lots of boys and girls go to boarding school. Obviously you would go to a good boarding school where you would get excellent teaching and play lots of games. Nicky is very good at cricket.'

'So am I,' Jamie replied. 'If you hurry, we can have a game.'

'What are we going to do about Jamie?' Jessica McEwan asked a few hours later as she stood staring out of the sitting-room window. 'So many couples in the world longing for a child, yet Lorne takes little notice of his only son.'

'How was he . . . before?' Laura asked.

Jessica twisted a cluster of rings around her finger. 'Anne never really told us what marriage to Lorne was like. I feel I can talk to you, Laura, about this very delicate situation. Somehow you've become part of this household as though you once lived here in another life. It's difficult to explain how completely you've fitted in. Take this morning, for instance. You seem to know what I'm talking about before I even say it. You know where to go to find things. You even echo my thoughts. It's uncanny. Little Jamie acts like he loves you already . . .'

'I feel at home here,' Laura said. 'Maybe it's magic.' She began to clip the loose typewritten sheets together. 'Whatever I can do to make you feel better, Miss Jessica, I'll do.'

'Jamie is waiting to go for his walk,' Jessica looked down at the aimlessly tumbling child. 'I can see we'll have to get him another governess or I'll have to fight him for your time.'

'What about a tutor?' Laura suggested. 'I take it Jamie has been giving his governesses a bad time?'

Jessica looked rueful. 'I think it all came about because of his terrible feeling of insecurity. For a long time he believed his mother had only left him and was coming back. Lorne, unhappily, didn't seem able to communicate with him. He was . . . is . . . too shattered himself. Tait has done nothing but help, but too much is left up to him. Then too, Tait had a strong love for his sister. Lorne doesn't seem to appreciate others are bereft.'

'You mustn't upset yourself, Jessica.' Laura came to the older woman and gestured to an armchair. 'Jamie is coming around. You said so yourself. I daresay Mr Sutton will too, in time. I think I can see Jamie with a tutor. He's such a strong-willed, definite little boy, he'd probably respond better to a man. There are plenty of well-educated young men out of a job. I'm sure there would be quite a few who would look on a stint out here as quite an adventure. Teaching Jamie wouldn't take up all of the time but I'm sure Tait would be glad of some help in the office.'

'I wonder . . .' Aunt Jessica said.

In the fortnight following Laura heard not a word about her proposal of a tutor for Jamie, but one late afternoon when she was working in the library, as usual, Tait came to the door.

'Good afternoon, Miss Kenmore,' he said. 'Hard at it, as usual?'

'That's right.' She flashed him an unruffled smile. 'Our work is coming along beautifully.'

'So Jessie tells me.' He moved a few papers and sat on the edge of the massive, Victorian desk. 'Would you like to come down and see if you can fix up Charlie?'

'He's still ill, is he?'

'I wish the whole bloody nonsense was over,' Tait said. 'I can't do anything, but I can't give up trying.'

'Mindji must be an expert sorcerer,' Laura said.

'It doesn't matter a damn if he is or he isn't,' Tait answered, 'the thing is, Charlie and all the rest of them believe he is. That's the power—the susceptibility to magic, black or white. Charlie found some white powder under his pillow this morning and this means he's in real trouble.'

'You can't mean this Mindji wants to see Charlie die?'

'If dying gets him out of the way, yes. Charlie has broken the expected code of behaviour. The men tell me he has been warned many times. Lily has been promised to Jacky since she was five. Custom can be departed from, but not in this case. Jacky wants her and his grandfather is determined on seeing he receives his bride.'

'Good God!' Laura looked sideways, out of the open French windows to the wide verandah beyond. 'One hears these things but one doesn't really believe it.'

'Believe it,' Tait returned a little harshly.

'Can't you find a mightier sorcerer than Mindji?' she asked seriously. 'Isn't there anyone who can counter the wretched old devil's magic with something potent of his own?'

'And just how would I get such a person on my side?' Tait looked down into smoky eyes. 'The fact of the matter is, Charlie has committed an offence. It ill becomes a man to look at another's promised bride.'

'You want to tell that to a few people I know,' Laura said wryly.

'This is another world, Laura,' Tait pointed out. 'Perhaps, even, the correct behaviour is more important to them than it is to us.'

'But love's the same for any colour.'

'It's love, is it?' he asked dryly. 'How do you know Charlie isn't simply lusting after Lily?'

'Can't they work it out themselves?'

'I wish to God they could.' His green eyes flashed brilliantly and he stood up and swung away from her—a leashed panther. 'Still, it's not a bad idea of yours,' he added. 'I might be able to persuade Father O'Neill at the Mission to arrange a little ceremony of his own. If he hadn't become a priest I'm sure he would have made a marvellous actor. The Irish have a way of talking not given to most people and he has been known to perform wondrous feats. The really outstanding one was bringing Paddy Mahoney back to life.'

'What?' Laura stared back at him in surprise.

'No easy feat when Paddy in his own words was "maggoty drunk". God knows what was in the incense but it earned Father O'Neill a reputation.'

'Truly?' She gave a delicious little gurgle.

'Do that again.'

'What?' In an instant they had jumped back into deep water.

He came back to her and put his hands upon her shoulders. 'Dear God, you're an alluring little witch.'

'Nothing to it if I just have to laugh.' She didn't realise the tell-tale colour was burning along her cheekbones, though she managed to keep her tone light.

'Jamie must have caught it from you. I hear him laughing all the time now.'

'I think up little things to amuse him.' Laura continued to sit with his hands resting on her shoulders trying to fight his overwhelming fascination. It seemed to emanate from him like a powerful beam.

'By the way,' he moved unhurriedly, 'I've organised a tutor for him. A young fellow not long out of university. His name is Peter Delprat. He's a cousin of friends of mine and apparently there's nothing he would like better than to spend a few hours a day teaching Jamie and the rest learning about station life. We'll give him a trial.'

'Have you told Jamie?'

His beautifully shaped mouth twitched. 'How could I even consider it without first telling you?'

'I hope Jamie likes the idea,' Laura gulped. 'He likes running wild.'

'Then I insist you break it to him first.' He moved over to one of the ceiling-high bookcases, adjusting a line of books that had fallen slightly sideways. 'Was it you, Laura, coming in search of *The Decline and Fall of the Roman Empire*?'

'I haven't touched anything there.'

'Oh?' He caught folds of white paper as they fell to the floor. 'What's this, I wonder?'

'Maybe the pages of a missing diary, though the paper looks new.'

Tait opened out the white cylinder and stood staring at the top sheet. 'My dear Miss Kenmore,' he said commandingly, 'come over here and see yourself.'

'You're joking!' Nevertheless Laura sprang up, going to his side.

At first she didn't even recognise herself in the pencilled heads, but he turned one after another; different attitudes, different expressions, like studies for a proposed portrait. It was her flowing hair, her eyes, her nose, her delicately determined chin. She didn't know she had that swan-like neck. There was a very soft, dreamy quality about the sketches, a very strange, exquisite tenderness.

'It's only someone who looks like me,' she said wonderingly.

'My dear Laura, save your breath.' His tone was so electric it crackled. 'I suppose you posed for these?'

'If they are me!' she cried.

'At least we have a mirror.' He seized her wrist and pulled her in front of an elaborately carved and gilded rectangular mirror atop an antique console.

Laura stood quite still, infinitely fair and feminine against his dark masculinity. Her composure scarcely lasted a minute, for he caught at the two combs in her hair and immediately it swirled down her neck, coming forward to touch one cheek, a few golden strands clinging to his hand.

'So?' Her eyes flew to his. 'You should be thrilled he has begun sketching again.'

'Why can't he sketch his son?'

'Perhaps he has.' She answered a little painfully. 'I can't explain this, Tait. It has nothing to do with me.'

'Lorne turns instinctively towards gentleness, comfort.'

'Who doesn't?' She remembered with sudden clarity the isolated moments over the past week when Lorne Sutton had sought her company.

'I don't,' he said bitingly. 'I have never needed, wanted, to drain a woman's strength.'

'Maybe your brother-in-law wants to be strong ...' She recoiled a little, bewildered. 'What is it, what's wrong?'

'You wouldn't understand.'

'I might if you tell me.'

He gave a harsh little laugh. 'What does Lorne talk to you about?'

'I see very little of him,' Laura said. 'Less than I do of you.'

'The fact is,' he returned tautly, 'he seems to have studied you enough to produce these.'

'Anyone would think I sat for hours!' Horribly she felt like crying. 'I don't understand why you're so angry. Surely he's an artist? He wanted to draw me and he did. Gosh, most artists draw women.'

'Why doesn't he draw Philippa?'

'She's not very kindly disposed towards him, you know.' Her agitation was showing in the darkening storm in her eyes.

'And you are?'

'I can feel for him,' Laura cried. 'That's my whole trouble. I can feel for lots of people. Even you.'

'And you'd do better to concentrate on me,' he told her shortly. 'Good advice no matter how disagreeable it sounds.'

'Let alone unthinkable and unpopular with some of your old g ... g ...' Laura was so angry she had to bite her tongue to stop herself.

'I-beg-your-pardon?' he asked icily.

'I'm sure you should.'

'What were you going to say?' He hauled her back to him.

'You're hurting me, Tait.'

'Don't be ridiculous.' He gritted his teeth.

'Laura, where are you?' Jamie came running in, slowing in amazement as he absorbed some of the atmosphere. 'Are you two fighting?' It was intolerable to see the dismay in his face.

'My dear little boy, I couldn't possibly fight with your uncle!' Laura cried convincingly.

'You looked funny.'

'We were having a very earnest discussion,' Tait said.

'About what?' Jamie moved across the room and grasped his uncle's hand.

'I suppose the time is ripe to get you a pony.'

'You mean it?' Jamie started to jump up and down.

'Laura was saying you would have to look after it.'

'Oh I would! I would, Laura. I'd be just so good. If you'd only let me have one.'

'Well . . .' Tait said presently. 'Of course we would have to speak to your father.'

'I expect he'll say no.' Jamie looked worried. 'Daddy doesn't care about ponies. He told some stupid woman that came to our place that he couldn't wait to get away from Mummy's horses.'

'Darling,' Laura shook his hand. 'That was just a little joke.'

'No it wasn't, I know. Mummy and Daddy had a fight about it afterwards. I hope you two never fight.'

'From the sound of that we can get married any time we like,' Tait murmured blandly. 'I have to go now, children. Laura has something else to tell you, Jamie. One more thing to help you along your way. Boys who rate ponies can't afford to ignore their lessons either.'

'If you say so, Uncle Tait,' Jamie piped up sweetly. 'I expect you mean another teacher. I won't screech or cry.'

'You're a good boy,' Laura added strongly.

'Yes, I'm a good boy.' Jamie looked up at her with his beautiful aquamarine eyes. 'You should tell Philippa that. She called me a little brat this morning.'

'And what did you say to her?' his uncle paused on his way to the door.

'I asked her why she didn't find another husband to look after her.'

'Jamie!' Laura moaned quietly.

'I want her to go.' Jamie smiled, a little uncertainly. 'It's our house. I don't know why she's always telling me to leave everything alone.'

'Guests, Jamie,' his uncle pointed out, 'deserve our courtesy.'

Jamie considered this and added another piece of information. 'Lamby said lucky she's got no children. She doesn't care about kids.'

'I feel sure, Jamie,' Laura told him, 'Philippa would care about her own. Perhaps you should remember she's not terribly happy.'

'That's right!' Jamie pondered, echoing another snippet from an overheard conversation. 'At least 'til she's got her man.'

A few days later Peter Delprat, an engaging and sensible young man, arrived and the household settled down to a set routine. Every morning at nine Peter came up from his allotted bungalow to begin Jamie's lessons, and the two of them moved off to the very schoolroom Jamie's McEwan great-grandfather had used. As Laura had predicted Jamie responded better to Peter's firm handling and after the first few mornings of subdued mumbles Jamie went off fairly happily. As Laura had discovered early, Jamie was a highly intelligent child and Peter had little trouble bringing him along. Jamie could read very well for a child his age and his pool of knowledge grew daily, much to Laura's and Aunt Jessica's delight. If Jamie's father noticed anything, he said nothing. Lorne had taken to coming to the dinner table now, making difficult conversation it was true, but this was looked upon as a great step forward by Jessica.

'We were absolutely petrified,' she confided in

Laura, 'that he was going to have a complete breakdown. You know, my dear, hospital. He was forever talking about "The Gates of Hell". Artists are quite different to the rest of us, as we quickly discovered. We all have our episodes of pure misery but we have to get through one way or another. When our darling Anne went into this marriage . . .'

'I know. I know.'

'She was the most loyal of creatures . . .'

Even then Aunt Jessica had been unwilling to discuss the hurtful rumours, and Laura more protective than ever, had not encouraged her to explore such a distressing subject. The Sutton marriage, it seemed, despite the high-profile public life, had not been a happy one. Perhaps Lorne Sutton's dramatic depression was related to guilt feelings, the despair of a man who believed he had somehow failed his young wife. There was all that talk about her turning to someone else. She was very beautiful. Laura had seen many of the glossy photographs, but somehow Anne Sutton had not looked like a woman who would act destructively. Everything Aunt Jessica and Mrs Lambert had told Laura about Jamie's mother had suggested the very opposite.

Laura's general impression of Lorne Sutton was that he was an extremely vulnerable person, susceptible to all kinds of emotional trauma. It was, she considered, an intense concentration of self, certainly such suffering left Jamie out in the cold. Perhaps this was at the core of ultimate despair, the feeling one suffered alone. No matter how desperate Laura had felt in those early terrible days after her parents had been killed, she had always had to manage for Nicky. She had always had the sense of responsibility for her brother. This was family and a powerful ally in the struggle. Lorne Sutton was just drifting, unrelated to his little son.

Aunt Jessica and Laura worked from nine through

to lunch, usually at one, and then again for an hour or so in the afternoon. It was an absorbing time for both of them, and Laura's evident interest in the unfolding Outback saga, *The Country of the Whirlwinds*, being connected to her other books, stimulated Jessica into making many changes in natural response to the quality of Laura's comments. She was, in fact, seeing her own work through the freshness of Laura's eyes and so much inspiration crowded in on her as she often remarked aloud to Laura: 'Where does one stop?'

For the most part, Laura wanted it all in. Someone had to record this unique way of life, the adventures and experiences; the accounts of the Aboriginal people as few white Australians knew them. With only a few weeks in the Outback Laura was already caught up in its powerful mystique. It was utterly different from anything she had ever known. Each morning she couldn't wait to walk out on to her little balcony looking out over the incredible view. From such a house one would expect to see acres of orderly gardens, perhaps a grand formality of plantings to balance the wonderful symmetry of the house, instead she was facing a mighty desert monument millions of years old. At dawn it was a sombre grape blue but as the sun illuminated the boundless plains it made a remarkable change to rose-pink. At midday it glowed a bright reddish-orange, then later on in the day according to the play of light it ranged from blue to purple. At sunset, Laura considered it was at its most magnificent, glowing like a burning coal from a fire. No matter what time she looked at it, it was never the same. For that matter it was never without its attendant eagle, soaring, hovering, diving for some unfortunate rock-dwelling marsupial.

The animal life was abundant and now after the unusual prolonged rains, the mesa like the vast surrounding plains, was covered with spinifex, mulga and a blinding brilliant array of wild flowers. Laura lived for the day when she could explore this mighty fortress. Though it lay at the very heart of the great station, from time to time the family granted access to certain well-credentialled photographers and writers, botanists and naturalists, and those deeply interested in the unique environment. A few experienced climbers, including Tait, had negotiated the steep sides of the gorges and reached the flat summit to look out over the great floodplains to the distant horizons. Laura yearned to do that but Tait had told her flatly she would have to content herself with exploring the honeycombed caves and rock shelters. To the Aborigines on the station and the nomads of the desert the island monument was steeped in legend. Here, Arrilka had taken shape from the mighty upheaval of the Dreamtime seabed. There were even marine fossils embedded in the sandstone cliffs.

'Tait must take you exploring this very weekend,' Aunt Jessica told her. 'It's marvellous to see a young person with such a great love of nature.'

Philippa was the only storm cloud in an otherwise cloudless cobalt. She had little or nothing to say to Laura, but in a house that size it was an easy matter to avoid one another. In any case Philippa seemed to ride out every day, looking as impeccable in her very close-fitting jodhpurs and silk shirts as she did in the cool, expensive things she wore in the evenings. Apparently she had a lot of very rich friends she could go to, but being at Eagle's Ridge was to be at peace. Or so she said. Laura had the feeling Philippa had never experienced *real* peace in her life. Beneath the exotic chill of her polished appearance, Philippa's soul seemed to be in the grip of demons.

'It's impossible to please her,' Mrs Lambert told Laura. 'She has to have this dish or that—all that low-calorie stuff—then when I go to great pains to make it edible she smiles in that pained way and leaves it. I say a good steak would make her look and act a whole lot better. Don't tell me that birdseed diet doesn't have a detrimental effect on the personality.'

For Mrs Lambert to have Laura as a confidante was a joy. She couldn't talk to the little housegirls—it would have been unthinkable to discuss the family with them—but Laura was somewhere between upper staff and family friend. Very soon Laura knew a great deal. There was nothing Mrs Lambert liked more than 'a good chat' though she always prefixed these enjoyable conversations with 'mind you, I'm not one to talk'.

Tait and Philippa had met in their late teens. Philippa's mother's second marriage was to a wealthy grazier (Philippa's father, the first husband, was never mentioned) and they had indeed been good friends for a number of years. Apparently the friendship had gone on for an unendurably lengthy period (Mrs Lambert was certain Mr Tait had never spoken of marriage) so rather than remain in a perpetual state of uncertainty Philippa took the plunge with 'a terribly nice chap, Jeff Winston-Hill'. Unfortunately poor Jeff had not remained alive very long—'mark my words the way she treated him was partly to blame'—so Philippa returned home where after a while she wasn't all that welcome (survival, Laura thought) so in a bitter huff with her mother she had begged to come to Eagle's Ridge.

Mrs Lambert felt it had reached the time when Philippa should be moving on. 'I thought maybe a week or so when she turned up, but she's been here for two months. You know what the Chinese say, dear.' Laura wasn't aware of that particular Chinese saying, so Mrs Lambert went on to inform her 'fish and guests go rotten after three days'.

'Of course never you, dear.'

'Gee, I'm glad.'

'We'd all miss you. Little Jamie has settled down marvellously. You've no idea the time he gave us for a while. But you seemed to win him over on sight. Then there's Miss Jessica, the love! Why, you look after her just like I do. I often think if I break a leg you could take over at a moment's notice.'

'I can't cook like you, Mrs Lambert,' Laura always said, wisely.

'Still—you'd manage. I know a domesticated little soul when I see one. Not like that Miss Philippa! All she's good for is dolling herself up.'

In the afternoons Laura and Jamie had their riding lessons. Although Laura loved horses for their great beauty she had never had the opportunity to learn to ride, so lessons were quickly arranged for her. Tait obviously could not afford the time and she imagined brilliant horseman that he was he wouldn't be all that tolerant, but a skilled instructor was detailed to work with Laura and the little boy.

There could never have been more enthusiastic pupils! Jamie was in seventh heaven with his pony, a beautiful creature with an ideal temperament (Jamie had called her 'Star' for the blaze on her forehead) and Laura, though she wasn't all that impressed with her mount at the start—for one thing it wasn't a magnificent looking animal like Tait's Wellington— she soon found it was plenty active enough. In fact her horse had been specially chosen, like Jamie's pony, for its sweet nature and kind heart. It was one thing to get the idea of the correct seat and quite another to hold it once the horse moved.

'You'll do, Miss Laura,' Scotty, their instructor, told her. 'Your muscles refuse to go the right way at first but you'll soon master it. The thing is practice. Work at it and work at it until the correct position comes naturally. You're using a whole lot of different muscles now.'

'I know that, Scotty, without being told.'

Jamie, on the other hand, had to be a natural rider because he almost fell into position.

'Great little chap that!' Scotty enthused. 'Look at it this way. He'd have to be wouldn't he? The Boss's nephew an' all. Miss Anne, now,' and here Scotty's eyes misted over, 'was a grand rider. You should have seen her and Mister Tait when they were nippers! So it doesn't surprise me young Jamie here is at home on a horse. Something wrong if he wasn't.'

If only Lorne would come down to check on Jamie's progress, but Lorne stayed away.

'He doesn't know what he's missing, does he, Laura?' a flushed Jamie told Laura as they marched down to the stables complex for their lesson. 'I'd really like to show him, but of course he'd never come. Why isn't Mummy here? Why isn't she, Laura?'

'Don't worry, Mummy can see you,' Laura tightened her grip on his hand.

'You mean she's up with God?'

'Peeping right over His shoulder to see what her little Jamie is doing.'

'Do you really think so, Laura?' Jamie looked up at her with his whole heart in his eyes.

'Yes, I really believe there's a point to it all, Jamie. Some people say there is no God, but we know about Him, don't we?'

Two big tears ran down Jamie's cheeks, and Laura's tender heart smote her. She stopped and sat down on the low stone wall, pulling Jamie on to her knee.

'Darling, don't cry now. Have I upset you?'

Jamie didn't answer but hugged her for a long time. His strong little arms clasped her around the neck and his tears dampened the thin cotton over her breast.

'Hush, sweetheart, hush.' She thought if he continued he would make himself ill. Certainly unable to have his riding lesson. 'You're not alone, are you? You have Daddy and Uncle Tait and Aunty Jessie. You have me. You're my best friend. And Jamie, you have Star. She's waiting for you, remember?'

For once Jamie didn't seem to care.

So it was, rounding the corner, that Tait came on them in the lovely classic embrace of child and woman.

'Hello, why aren't you down at the stables? I've come back all this way to see how you're both getting on.'

Laura had lifted her head and he read in her eyes and the poignancy of her expression that this was one of those moments Jamie was desperately missing his mother. Nevertheless he said cheerfully: 'Right-o, Jamie, do you still like a piggy-back?'

Jamie, tear-stained, looked up immediately. 'I do, Uncle Tait.'

'Well, you're bigger that's for sure, but I think I can still carry you.'

It was settled. Jamie wanted a piggy-back and soon his tears were completely set aside.

After dinner that night Laura forced herself to approach Lorne Sutton.

'Ah, Laura.' He had been sitting almost peacefully, contemplating the millions of dazzlingly clear stars, when Laura moved out on to the verandah.

'May I speak to you, Mr Sutton?'

'Lorne, please,' he corrected her. 'After all, I've been calling you Laura for some time.'

'Thank you.' She refused the rattan armchair he advanced for her and gestured towards the garden. 'Could we take a walk?'

'I'd like to.' He unwrapped his long legs. It had not escaped his attention that she was looking very earnest. 'It's about Jamie, isn't it?'

'Yes.' She preceded him slightly down the wide flight of steps. 'You know, of course, that we're having riding lessons?'

'Here we go again,' he said oddly.

'Has someone else spoken to you?' She turned her shining head, her yellow dress in the glimmering light a rich splash of colour.

'Tait.'

'Oh.'

'You must have known he would bring it up, Laura. I admire Tait enormously. He has been the best brother-in-law a man could wish for, a solid rock, always utterly in control, and he does so make me feel ineffectual.'

So what are you going to do about it? Laura thought. In a way Lorne Sutton sounded like he blamed Tait for being so strong.

'You realise I'm not a horsey person at all, Laura,' he was now saying.

Then you married into the wrong family. 'But then, Lorne,' Laura pointed out gently, 'Jamie only wants to show you something he excels at. He's really very good indeed.'

'So I've been told.' He laughed briefly, a faintly rasping sound. 'I guess I hoped for a talented child.'

'He is talented.' Laura could hardly believe it. 'I'm sure he'll make a splendid horseman one day. He could even represent his country one day at the Olympic Games. Scotty thinks he's marvellous and Peter Delprat must have told you he's highly intelligent. A very promising little boy.'

'When I was his age,' Lorne Sutton looked up at the sky, 'I was already impressing people with my drawings.'

'That's funny. My parents used to be pretty impressed with my drawings too.'

'You sound a little angry, Laura.' He stopped, looking down at her, genuinely taken aback.

'You wish Jamie had inherited your special gift, is that it?'

'How crisp you are, my dear.'

'I've become very fond of Jamie, Mr Sutton ... Lorne.'

'Yes, you have been frightfully good to him.'

'He's very sweet and very strong.'

'Why not, he's half-McEwan. In fact he's so like Tait he could be his child.'

'Instead he's yours,' Laura pointed out very delicately. 'He loves you and misses you, you must know that?'

'I . . .' Lorne's cultured voice drifted away and his dark, thin face looked quite stricken.

'I know the awful time you've had.' Laura tried to ease that look of misery.

'How could you?'

'I've told you before. I lost my parents.'

'Parents are rather different to a wife. Anne loved me so much. We were so happy when we got married, though it's a mystery to me even now how we got together. Anne was first and last a countrywoman. She was bred to all this—this appalling, lonely grandeur. I mean it's like a crazy fairytale, a huge, great mansion chockablock with treasures in an empty desert. Take Tait, even. He lives like a king in some inaccessible kingdom. Good God, it's an extraordinary way of life. He thinks nothing of owning one of the biggest stations on earth, having thousands of square miles to himself.'

'Aren't you forgetting stations like Eagle's Ridge are the mainstay of the beef industry?' Laura tried to keep her voice calm.

'Yes, I see that, but honestly these people are different.'

'You don't want Jamie to follow his uncle's lead?'

'What?' He looked down at her astonished.

'I said . . .'

'Yes, I heard what you said, Laura. You're very direct.'

'I suppose I am.' She caught a flower, leaned sideways and sniffed in its glorious perfume. 'It's not my intention to offend you in the slightest way. I can understand you're a little disappointed Jamie doesn't draw as you did when you were a child. Which is not to say he mightn't attempt it at some time.'

'I don't think it's something you learn,' Lorne Sutton murmured regretfully. 'It's simply something one can do. I suppose you haven't seen any of my work?'

'Indeed I have,' Laura walked on. 'I can't think

there would be many people interested in art who haven't. You're a wonderfully gifted man.'

'How nice for you to say it.'

'I'm sure you hear it all the time.'

'That's true, but it actually means something coming from you.'

Laura was glad of the dark because she could feel herself abruptly flushing.

'I was going to ask you something, Laura,' Lorne Sutton said.

'Will it be difficult?' She tried a light note.

'I hope not.' Unexpectedly he caught her hand, swinging her around to face him. 'Would it be too much bother for you to pose for me?'

'That's a very great compliment,' she murmured diplomatically. Now what else could she say?

But Lorne took this as assent. He sighed deeply and his face lightened. 'I've been quite unable to work. This place ... the pain in me ... it has been an extraordinarily hard time.'

'Yes.' Laura felt very, very wary.

'Thank you so much, my dear,' he said softly. 'It won't be anything complicated. You have marvellous skin to paint.'

It was altogether harrowing and Laura tried to reason out why. Lorne Sutton was a very highly regarded artist. She should be honoured she had reinspired him to paint, instead she felt unable to cope with the possible repercussions.

'If I promise to sit for you,' she bargained with him point blank, 'would you promise to come down to the stables and see how Jamie is going with his riding lessons?'

'If I must, Laura.' He had a very attractive drawl but Laura would have changed it for a very ocker, definite yes.

'Then you couldn't do better than come tomorrow. It will be a special occasion for Jamie.'

'I hope for you, too, Laura,' he said, and very gently

ran one finger down her cheek.

Laura was stunned. She had no idea what that gesture meant. It had a terrible touch of sensuousness in it, when she had been led to believe Lorne Sutton was in deep mourning for his wife. It would be a terrible thing if he was now starting to look at another woman. Men were notorious for their acts of disloyalty.

Maybe she was crazy altogether. He was much older. He thought her a kind and sympathetic young woman. How could she judge him in her rash, woman's way? Still, his finger had lingered against her skin. It wasn't pleasant but just a little creepy. The fatal moves people made. How was she supposed to interpret it? Laura's heart beat accelerated and she put her hand to her throat. Tait would strangle her.

CHAPTER SEVEN

IT came as no surprise to her to find Tait McEwan ranged against one of the white columns awaiting their return.

'I shouldn't be surprised if we get a late storm,' he said.

'It's very still.' Laura knew she sounded apologetic.

'Storms are nice.' Loren Sutton sighed almost happily. 'I suppose I should return your cassette recorder to you, Laura.'

'Not if it's working.'

'Oh, it is.' Somehow he had undergone an enormous transformation, for oddly he had regained a lot of his old attraction. 'It was a lovely thought.'

'I'm glad.' And she was.

'Well, I'll see you both in the morning,' he looked affectionately at his brother-in-law then back at Laura. 'I'm tempted to start a little work tonight.'

'Sketching?' Tait asked slowly.

'That's right.' His black eyes were suddenly brilliant. 'Seeing Laura has consented to sit for me.'

'You, funny-face?' Tait asked, and straightening up towered over Laura.

'She's lovely!' Lorne responded rather intensely. 'Those fine delicate bones and that flawless creamy skin. You have no idea how difficult it is to paint skin. So I'll be off.'

'It's kind of unbelievable isn't it?' Laura hazarded after he had gone.

'I'd be praying for something but I assure you this wasn't it.' Tait answered a little savagely. 'What in God's name persuaded you to go walking with him?'

'You do that frightfully well,' she said.

'What?' His green eyes were glittering like jewels.

'The frowning tyrant.'

'Don't try to be smart at my expense.'

'I'm not trying to be smart, I'm merely parrying the thrust.'

'Which is one and the same thing. Don't go in yet,' he said crisply.

'Shall we sit down or go for a walk?' Laura marvelled at herself for so provoking him.

'We might be obliged to walk,' he returned acidly.

'Have you seen someone I have not? Perhaps, Philippa?'

'You are a one, aren't you?' He took a firm grip on her arm and all but compelled her down the steps.

'Why don't we go for a drive?' she flashed a look at him. 'I've done my share of walking for the night.'

'Why not?' he answered crisply, keeping his hold on her. 'I have the odd feeling Lorne is standing out on the balcony watching what we're doing.'

'I fancy Philippa might be too.' The queerest excitement was loosening her tongue. 'Do you still fancy her?'

'I never did.'

'That's not what I've heard.'

He was angry; there was no doubt about that. 'Do you really think you should be gossiping with the staff?'

'Of course. How else am I going to find anything out?'

'Perhaps even write about it?'

'No.' She flinched instinctively. 'I gave you my word.'

'It's just your habit to be provocative.' They had come along the side of the house to the huge, white-painted outbuilding that housed station vehicles, including motor bikes and a good deal of machinery and Laura looked up at him in surprise.

'Are we really going for a drive?'

'You sound as old as Jamie.' For the first time his hard expression relaxed.

'I was only having a little joke.' Every nerve in her body seemed to be leaping and she hoped fervently that he wasn't aware of his devastating effect on her. This banter was only a veneer to cover the sexual currents beneath the surface. If she was so very strongly attracted to him, surely he would like to make love to her? She could even understand the way they conducted their conversations with humour or mockery and always an underlying challenge.

'Frightened, Laura?' His voice reflected her very thoughts.

'A few considerations are giving me pause.'

'You've never done this before?'

'I'm sure you have.'

'Of course I have.' He laughed. 'It's no secret quite a few beautiful girls have come my way.'

'And you never wanted to marry one of them?' He was holding the door of a jeep open and she climbed into the seat.

'I thought marrying might spoil things.'

'It seems to in lots of cases.' Could she really keep up the flippancy? Her heartbeats were shaking her.

They drove out of the huge barn and headed away from the main compound to the vast expanse of spinifex country. The stars were incredible; not glimmering as in the city but possessed of a size and brilliance that enchanted the eye. The purple heavens were as densely sown with them as the plains were sown with flowers and from some native night-camp came the now familiar sound of the possum-skin drums giving tongue.

Laura lifted her face to the swiftly rushing night wind. The air was surprisingly cool after the heat of the day and the tyres of the jeep were crushing the aromatic grasses and the sweet-scented carpet of wild flowers, stirring the blood with bush fragrance.

'This is marvellous!' She stretched up her arms like some primitive goddess.

'You're not cold?'

'No.' Now she clasped her arms around her. 'If you won't take me exploring this weekend I'm going to ask Peter.'

'You should.'

'All right.' She couldn't quite conceal her acute disappointment.

'I'll take you, Laura,' he told her lazily. 'I couldn't miss it.'

'Are we going anywhere in particular?' she called to him, making ineffectual efforts to control her whipping hair.

'There's a particular waterhole about two miles from here where the brolgas congregate. The brolgas, you know, are our blue cranes.'

'You mean we might see them dance?' She had heard numerous stories about the brolgas' ballets.

'I can't guarantee it but it's not unusual to see them perform.'

'I've seen them flying with the acres of budgies and touching down with all those funny little running steps but dancing must be a magical sight.'

'Well, we'll see.' He glanced at her swiftly. 'You're in a bit of bother with your hair.'

'If I'd known we were going to come I'd have brought a scarf.'

'Why worry,' he said dryly. 'From here you look dazzling.'

Glancing back Laura could see they had come quite a distance from the house. The homestead was a blaze of lights, like a luxury liner riding a midnight ocean. She wondered if Lorne Sutton had really been watching them and what Philippa might be thinking now.

Coolibahs ringed the deep waterhole, growing out of the silvery sand.

'Keep your head down,' he told her as he guided her down a narrow path that led to the water.

'Oh heck!' An owl hooted and she slammed into him with fright.

'Can you possibly wait for me to grab you.'

'You know that owl startled me.'

'Hush, keep your voice down. If you move too fast or talk too loudly all the birds will desert us.' His own voice was barely above a whisper.

'I'm sorry.'

He held her hand and they moved stealthily through the blossoming thicket.

'I can't see anything.'

'Are you going to shut up?'

The waterhole lay ahead of them, a fair-sized body of water, its mirror-smooth surface a secret silver in the glimmering light.

'Maybe they won't come at all?'

'You couldn't keep quiet if you tried.'

'I'm only whispering.' Her eyes were adjusting to the softly glowing light. Some feathery little trees, perhaps acacias, bent their long tresses over the water upstream. There appeared to be a bend in the billabong, indeed the waterhole was much larger than she had thought. Clumps of ferns resembling maidenhair tickled her slender feet in her thin sandals. She hoped the ferns didn't conceal any tiny little animals, or worse, frogs. He would never forgive her if she shrieked.

'This is beautiful,' she breathed. 'I've never done anything so mad in my life.'

'I suppose only one thing will shut you up.' He swerved and took her by the elbows.

'Don't you dare kiss me,' she exclaimed passionately.

'What you're saying is you enjoy it too much. I've a very fine instinct about such things.

'And I'm a person. Not a body.'

'I haven't forgotten.' He was faintly smiling, his mouth curved in such a way all of a sudden her heart turned over.

'Don't, Tait.'

He gathered her into his arms, holding her tight. 'I won't bite you, only nibble those soft lips a little.'

'Why?'

'Why do you think?' He lowered his head and traced the outline of her mouth with the tip of his tongue.

Oh God, she thought. Oh, God.

He arched her body back a little and kissed her throat. Her yellow dress was sleeveless with a softly draped cross-over bodice and she felt his mouth trail down the deep V so she was inhaling deeper and deeper each time. Her eyes had fluttered closed and she felt so weak he was half-supporting her.

'Have you ever had a lover?' he murmured almost dreamily.

'Uhmm.' She tilted her head back exposing her full throat to him.

He gripped her powerfully.

'Not yet,' she told him. 'Why do you want to know?'

'Because I'm determined to be the first.'

'You must be mad. Mad . . . mad . . .' She tried to turn her head but now he caught up her mouth, kissing her so hungrily she responded uncontrollably. It was impossible not to know he wanted her, her imprisoned body moulded to his taut thighs.

'You're so beautiful . . . so real . . . so much a woman!' His hand came down over her breast, his long fingers spearing beneath her light bra to find the creamy flesh.

She seemed to be panting with desire, gasping aloud as thumb and forefinger manipulated the naked nipple to an exquisite peak. She knew she moaned with the pleasure, melting closer, so now his touch that had had a caressing delicacy lost its fine control. The hand that swept her shoulders and the upper curves of her breasts was forceful and possessive, as though nothing could stand between him and the urgency of his need.

He was kissing her harder, deeper, opening up a whole world of sensuality that made every considera-tion fly from her mind. It was almost as though he couldn't get enough of her, and though she wanted to give him everything she was oddly frightened. He

seemed immensely more powerful, more able to
contend with this radiant excitement.

'Tait!' she pleaded, managing to pull her face away
slightly.

'Don't.' He enfolded her again, feeling her shudder
as his mouth travelled over her face. 'Why, Laura,' his
voice went very deep and husky, 'you're crying.'

'I'm not.'

'You are.' There was a strange wonder in his tone.
'Did you think I was going to ravish you?'

'I didn't think I could stop you.'

'You're so . . . perfect to make love to. I want you
naked.' He licked the tears from her face.

'There's no end to what you want.'

'Who's around to see us?' He kissed her closed eyes.

'Anyway the answer's no,' she whispered.

'I believe I can change that.'

'I believe you won't try.'

He threw up his head, then stared down at her. 'Do
you know how many restless nights you've cost me
since you've been here?'

'Me?' her eyes flew open in shock.

'Uhmm, you.' His voice crisped. 'Don't give me
that searching, sweet-little-innocent stare. You're the
best when it comes to turning on the charm.'

'I'm no different to anybody,' she said.

'You don't play at provoking me?' His shapely
mouth turned down.

'You know I'm not serious.' Her silvery eyes
widened.

'Then you're playing games with the wrong man. I
always get what I want, Laura, more or less.'

'Then I assure you you've got the wrong girl. I
come from a particularly good background . . .'

'You'd practically forgotten it.' His velvety voice
was sardonic.

'I guess you know I'm attracted to you.'

'Yes, quite a bit. Don't get so agitated. I'm only
going to kiss a tiny little corner of your mouth.'

She trembled so violently he moved back to gentleness, his mouth closing over hers with a voluptuous slowness.

She tried to fight the ravishing sweetness but she couldn't and he continued to kiss her for a long while, not touching her breasts, but contenting himself with the leisurely exploration of her mouth.

'Enough,' she whispered. 'Tait, I can't stand up.'

'I suppose it's too dangerous to lie down?'

'Anyway we must go back.'

'Would it make any difference if I said I'd think about marrying you?' He spoilt it all by laughing.

'It really wouldn't make a difference.'

'You appalling little liar. I'm the best catch you could ever find.'

Just as she thought this limb-melting languor would go on forever there was the rustle of many wings. Large wings, beating silkily, then an eerie, running patter.

'The bro . . .'

He put his hand over her mouth.

It was a very effective way to hush her. The birds were coming from upstream; silvery grey in the ghostly light, ready to begin their legendary ceremony. Laura was reminded that the brolgas' famous ballets formed the basis of the most beautiful native dances and now as she stood enraptured the large, four-feet high cranes arranged themselves in a set pattern, their reddish crests like small crowns. This was a magic lake and soon the graceful birds would turn into slender nymphs with eyes like great pools of shadowed light.

There was no sound from her now. Laura stood within the circle of Tait McEwan's locked arms as the brolgas began their slow sacred dance. She would have thought perhaps the definite choreography of these ballets had been exaggerated yet right before her very eyes blue cranes were bowing and bending, stepping out their stately measures . . .

It was mesmeric. The very air seemed to join in the

performance, the breeze coming with a melodic
soughing, so as well as being very beautiful the
performance was faintly eerie. There were six birds in
all and they moved to their partners just as the dancers
did in human ballets. What made these beautiful
creatures behave this way? What directed them to
dance?

'Has Jamie seen this?' She put back her head and
whispered very close to Tait McEwan's mouth.

'No.' He took advantage of her position straightaway
and kissed her, so it wasn't long before she turned into
his arms. The magic was so absolute; such a blend of
mystery, ancient ritual, and a half-fearful rapture. She
had never experienced emotions remotely like it
before.

It was Tait, in fact, who broke their passionate
embrace, a fantastic feat of self-control because Laura
had been meeting his demands with unreserved
ardour.

'Oh, you've stopped.'

'God, little one, I've got to stop.'

'The brolgas, the birds——' She became suddenly
agitated, looking around and as she did so the birds,
disturbed, broke their precise ranks and paced away in
alarm. Laura had expected them to fly, taking off as
they did with the curious vibrating sound of their
great wings, but perhaps they really were enchanted
nymphs for they hurried along the silver sand and
quickly lost themselves in the pitch-black bush.

'They're human. You know they are,' Laura said.

'The Aboriginal legends are not unlike the story of
Swan Lake. Now, Miss Kenmore, I'm going to get
you home. Say what you like, a beautiful woman is
fundamentally a sex-symbol.'

They argued about that all the way home and just as
Laura was starting to lose her temper, he enclosed her
determined little chin in his hand and said: 'I'm only
fooling, sweet one.'

'I thought you had to be,' she sighed.

'I just like to get you going. You've no idea how
fluent you've been.'

Laura found she couldn't let go of him even in her
sleep. The scent of him clung to her; the touch of his
mouth and his hands. It was almost like having him
with her in the bed. Almost.

About two o'clock the storm broke and Laura sat up
abruptly in shocked amazement. That had to be the
most powerful clap of thunder she had ever heard in
her life. Now thoroughly awakened she was dazzled by
the answering flash of lightning then the bombardment
began again. God, it must have sounded like this
thousands of years ago, she thought gaspingly and
jumped up to go to her balcony.

A great bolt of lightning flashed and the world went
white. She cowered instinctively, the sight of Arrilka
burning itself into her eyeballs in stark grandeur.
Tonight the flat-topped mountain was dead black,
thrown into shocking relief against the vast white
expanse of electrified sky.

Perhaps she would be wise to go in. That clap of
thunder almost jolted her off her feet, cracking across
the sky like a celestial whip.

'Laura!'

As the din momentarily subsided, she heard the
pitiful little cry.

'That's my poor little Jamie!' Laura exclaimed
aloud and raced across to her door.

To her surprise she couldn't see Jamie at all until
Jamie confirmed his position on the floor. He was
sitting all huddled up, his hands clapped over his ears.

'Jamie, pet!' She was a slender girl but she picked
him up.

'The lightning, it's dangerous!'

'It can't hurt us in here.'

'Please, can I come in with you. I'll be so good.'

'Of course, darling. I was going to dash down and
see how you were anyway.'

'Do you suppose we could shut the French windows?'

'If you want to, dear, but the rain will start soon and the thunder and lightning will stop. Which reminds me, your French windows. Are they still open?'

'Sure, Laura. I didn't touch them.' Jamie tumbled almost happily now on to the bed. 'Turn on the light.'

'Hey, listen, young man, this isn't going to turn into a party.'

'I was hoping you'd get me a drink.'

'What kind of a drink?'

'Lemonade?'

'I can't do that.'

'Water?'

'Yes, a glass of water is wonderful sometimes.'

Laura switched on her bedside lamps and the lovely room sprang to life.

'I love your bed, Laura,' Jamie said admiringly, his small terrors forgotten.

'It's very grand, isn't it? A fairy-tale four-poster.' The rain was starting to fall, heavy and driving and without being checked it would have come into the room. Laura jumped back slightly as her nightgown was spattered with heavy drops. 'There, that better?' she asked Jamie as she pulled the doors shut. 'I can't close the shutters, I'll get drenched.'

'No, that's all right, Laura,' Jamie nodded, and looked at her. 'You look so pretty with the rain like little diamond beads.'

'Why, thank you, Mr Sutton,' she smiled at him in faint surprise. They started early these McEwan-Suttons. 'Will you be all right if I dash down to your room for a minute? I'll have to close your doors.'

'Hurry, Laura.' Jamie took over two of her pillows for his own. 'Gee, this smells like scent.' He buried his little nose in the beruffled pink pillow.

'Won't be long.' Laura waggled her fingers at him and went quickly to the door, shutting it quietly before racing down the dark corridor. The rain whipped at her again as she swiftly closed Jamie's

French windows and she tried to brush the drops away with her palms. Diamond beads, indeed. That wasn't bad for a five-year-old.

She was almost at Jamie's door when a tall, black figure materialised. Very male. Very powerful.

'Who's that?' she mouthed almost soundlessly.

'Laura?'

The figure advanced a few paces and grabbed her.

'Oh, gosh, Tait, it's you. You're one heck of a big man.' All the willpower in the world couldn't stop her from bending over a little in reaction.

'Are you all right?' He still held her with one hand, the other smoothing back her damp hair.

'Of course I am.'

'Jamie?' He looked past her to the bed.

'He's in my room. The thunder and lightning frightened him.'

'I thought it might. He's not yet used to storms in our part of the world. Come along, let's fetch him.'

She shook back her hair. 'Let him stay with me.'

'How about if I stay with you tomorrow night?' He switched on the light and looked at her. He was wearing a black silk robe and for all she knew nothing else and now she could see herself through his eyes. She had not bothered to pull on her robe and if her nightgown wasn't sheer, it nevertheless was a very revealing garment. In fact his hand came out and brushed along her collarbone, transmitting passion in one instant powerful message. 'I could crush you.'

'I have to go back to Jamie,' she whispered.

Stunningly he scooped her up and she gave an incoherent little gasp, then began to caution him severely.

'You put me down this minute.'

'Do as you're told for once, okay?'

If only ... if only ... if only ... the force of her own desire startled her. 'I have to go back to little Jamie.'

'So do I, darling.' His voice was almost tender but as ever laced with humour. 'Jamie may think he's in for a delicious night in a soft bed with his lovely Laura, but I'm going to take him back with me.'

'Oh, Uncle Tait!' Jamie cried out delightedly, as they moved into Laura's room. 'Did the storm wake you up?'

'I wasn't sleepy, my lad. You look very comfortable there.'

'Hmmm!' Jamie snuggled up. 'Don't worry about me now.'

'What about if I find you a spot in my bed?' Tait suggested. 'We'll be two guys bunking in.'

Jamie lifted himself on his elbow. 'What does Laura think?'

'It ought to be friendly.' She smiled.

'Did you really come to see about me, Uncle Tait?' Jamie asked.

'Sure did, Jamie,' his uncle agreed. 'Storms take a bit of getting used to out here.' His gleaming green eyes moved to Laura. 'I was going to look in on Laura as well.'

'Why don't we all go back together?' Jamie happily suggested.

'It's not the done thing, old chap.'

'Only Mummys and Daddys sleep together?'

'That's the idea.' Tait leant over and ruffled his nephew's shiny, tousled curls. 'Are you sure you were frightened of the storm?'

'I'm much better now,' Jamie said proudly. 'The first big thunder made me fall off the side of the bed.'

'Well, don't fret, you'll be all right now. Reckon you can walk?'

'Of course I can.' Jamie gurgled. 'Laura has such a struggle trying to hold me.'

'So what male is so helpless?' Laura laughed. There was so much love and tenderness in Tait McEwan's expression as he looked down at his small nephew she thought it rather heart-stopping in such a big, tough man. 'You need children of your own, you know,' she said softly. 'You're surprisingly good with them.'

'Why surprisingly?' He lifted one beautifully marked brow.

'You should see yourself when you're mad.'

'My dear girl, I don't think you have.'

'Uncle Tait, you've got bare toes!' Jamie shook his uncle's hand.

'So have you. So has Laura. What did you expect, evening dress?'

Jamie staggered with laughter, with face pink with merriment and his eyes faintly glazed. 'This is fun, isn't it, in the middle of the night?'

'So we'd better get you to bed.' Tait suddenly swooped and picked the child up.

'Come with us, Laura. Tuck me in.'

Laura shook her head, not quite sure.

'All you have to do, Miss Kenmore, is walk in and walk out.' His green eyes were positively glittering with malicious enjoyment. The black silk robe fell back to reveal his darkly tanned, powerful chest and Laura found herself with the urge to slip her hand beneath the lapels. His shoulders were very wide, yet his hips were very lean. It was a wonderfully athletic body altogether.

Jamie was only in the massive English four-poster a few moments before his eyelids began to fall. 'Night, night, Laura,' he murmured sleepily. 'I can't do any schoolwork tomorrow, I'm too tired.'

'He can have a sleep-in at that,' Tait decided. 'You have a perfectly good opportunity now, Laura, to do what you wanted to do before.'

'I'm sorry, I don't quite know what it was.' She almost scurried to the door. It was rather a long way for it was a perfectly enormous room, the sort of master bedroom not even the rich could afford these days.

He joined her in the softly glimmering dark outside his door. 'You looked to me like you wanted to move your hand over my body.'

'It's the robe,' she hissed. 'You can see it's a great big come-on.'

'Is it?' He laughed in his throat. 'And to think I never considered that.'

'Good night, Mr McEwan,' she said firmly.

'I suppose it would be a kindness to allow you to feel my shoulder.' He took her hand, which abruptly turned powerless, and moved it across the hard wall of his chest.

'All right, you've had your bit of fun,' she whispered shakily.

'Hell, this isn't fun at all. It's torture.'

Perhaps it was but it was extraordinarily erotic. The sensitised tips of her fingers swept the velvety warmth of his shoulders, tangled in the dusky matt of hair. She could feel the steady thud of his heart, though hers seemed to have stopped.

'You're the very devil of a man,' she stared upwards into his gleaming eyes. 'I don't think I could ever trust a man with a cleft chin.'

'Would you sleep with him?'

'I might want to, but I wouldn't.'

'You require a marriage proposal first.' His low voice was soft and mocking.

'I require a marriage certificate!' Her fingers tightened on a little curl of black chest hair and she tugged slightly. 'But not from you, Mr McEwan. Don't let yourself think that.'

'Oh yes I can, Laura.' He was very close to her now, locking his arms about her waist. 'You do want to sleep with me. In fact, there's going to come a time when you will allow it.'

Her skin seemed to be superheated, on fire, but she pushed hard against his chest, arching her back against his locked arms. 'What happened to all your lady friends?'

He lifted her hand and pressed the palm to his mouth. 'I expect they all got married.'

'A girl can't wait forever. Don't you think it's time

you made a commitment? You can't enjoy this *droit du seigneur* much longer.'

His handsome dark face was in deep shadow. 'Would you have my child?' he asked abruptly.

It upset her; the question and the oddness of his tone. Such talk was too disturbing, too deeply personal. It cut close to the heart.

'Let me go, Tait.'

'I can't let you go.' It didn't sound mocking or lover like, but hard and determined.

'I can't take this. I really can't.' She hung her blonde head. 'I'm not one to joke about intimacy.'

'And I'm an irresponsible womaniser,' he returned acidly. 'Still you're being a bit premature talking love and marriage. I want you. That's all I said.'

'And that's enough?' She threw up her head, silvery eyes flashing. 'You know the trouble with you? You've been too indulged.'

'My dear girl,' he said cuttingly, 'you can't know the life I've had.'

'That's right! I don't know. I can't know. This whole conversation is ridiculous.'

'Yes, and you're feeling very sorry for yourself and not safe. You can fume as much as you like, but you're awfully susceptible to me. In fact you're more frightened of yourself than you are of me.'

'Seducer,' she said softly.

'If I were, I would have seduced you, Laura.' He bent his head and briefly kissed her mouth. 'Mutual consent is what I like and clearly not that far out of reach.'

The rain was still falling when Laura opened her French windows, but the worst of the storm was over. The air was miraculously clean and fresh and strangely as tangy as the breeze off surf. No matter how far back one had to go in prehistory, 600 million years, there were moments when one was reminded of the primaeval inland sea. Even the rock formations had curious wave-like patterns.

It was many long moments before her heartbeats slowed. Each encounter she had with Tait became increasingly shattering. She had thought herself fairly sophisticated, yet she could do nothing about her helpless response to his lead. He had only to look at her, touch her. He drew her too frighteningly easy. Sometimes she almost dared to tell herself she was in love with him only it could be an immense mistake. Their real lives were in two different worlds. He was in perfect control of his, whereas she had to fight for survival.

Then there was Nicky. She found herself aching to see him. She had to watch over Nicky until he was ready to stand on his own two feet. Years yet. Years. When she had explained once to an ardent admirer that she would always have Nicky to look after his momentarily unguarded face had displayed dismay. He had even told her she was in much the same position as a single woman with a child; the child being an enormous handicap. Their pleasant relationship had not survived. Love me. Love my brother. Not everyone was filled with a protective generosity. Yet she knew a man like Tait McEwan was infintely generous. It charmed her to watch him with Jamie . . . so much about him she had learnt to admire. And no one, no one, had unlocked such desire. Whether she ever spoke of it or not, there was no doubt that she was in love with him . . . loved him . . . what was the difference? Why ever had he asked her if she would have his child? Until that very moment it had not occurred to her that she would love that above all.

CHAPTER EIGHT

OVER Easter the house was filled with guests, but only one really mattered to Laura. In a handful of months Nicholas had grown inches, not only in stature but in the strengthening and maturing of his character. The heightened vulnerability and bouts of weeping and depression linked to the shocking trauma of losing his parents had at last subsided and with the resilience of youth and the help of Uncle Clive and boys' school at its best, Nicholas was developing into the sort of young man his sister hoped and prayed for. Not everyone had it in them to withstand and triumph and Laura had endured many agonised moments reflecting on the possible psychological effects Nicky might suffer growing up without a mother and father.

Until she had made the decision to send him to Uncle Clive he had been excessively attached to her (which she thought normal) and although there was always to be the deepest loving bond between them, it was clear Nicky was coming into his own. A most encouraging sign. He greeted the family with warmth, respect and gratitude and a considerable amount of boyish charm (shades of Daddy, Laura thought) and Jamie took to him much in the certain way he had taken to Laura; in fact an extension of family. Laura and Nicky were remarkably alike, with the same elegant bone structure and ultra-blond colouring, but whereas Laura was very quick in everything she did with almost a redhead's volatility, Nicky was more placid and steady, with a good deal of natural caution to his sister's impulsiveness. Both had sunny natures, warm and friendly, but Laura was the far more complex of the two.

Over that marvellous long weekend the sight and

sound of Nicky so obviously well and happy filled her with an enormous tranquillity. Tait and Aunt Jessica (Philippa assumed the role of junior hostess) were kept busy entertaining their guests so Laura, the two boys and Peter Delprat roamed the great station in perfect freedom, enjoying all it had to offer.

'This is super!' Nicky was heard to breathe at least one hundred times. The sun had very quickly tanned him golden and his eyes were extraordinarily brilliant. He had never ridden a horse before, taken part in a muster, watched branding and roping and range bred horses broken in. He had never been up in a helicopter looking down at one of the biggest cattle stations on earth and he had never seen anything so fantastic as Arrilka or the astonishing sight of the vast flood plains covered in wild flowers.

'I thought it would be barren!' he cried. 'But this is fantastic!'

Every single day he was alive with excitement. He never knew billy tea and camp damper could taste so good. He never knew stockmen had such marvellous tales to tell or old tribal witch doctors could be so frightening. Swimming in the surf was hard to beat but he soon developed a taste for Outback lagoons where one could play Tarzan, and like everyone else who visited the Outback he was entranced by the birdlife. When he thought of a single little budgie in a cage when out here the great clouds of them blocked out the sun. Once they saw a hawk swoop leisurely down on a flock of crimson chats feeding on the ground and Jamie and Nicky had run hotly to the spot clapping their hands so the thousands of small birds could take to the air and escape.

Arrilka's attendant eagle could be easily identified, its great seven-foot wing span curving upwards, its three-inch talons at the ready should some medium-sized kangaroo present itself when this magnificent bird of prey was hungry. Then there were the glorious parrots, the pink and grey galahs, and millions of white corellas that lived in the tree-lined watercourses. The lignum swamps were full of birds, ibis, shags, spoonbills and herons and the whistling tree ducks. They never saw the pelicans because they bred on islands in the remote swamps where Tait didn't want them to go. Wild pigs could be a hazard but the dingos were unlikely to bother them. A wild dingo in prime condition was a marvellous sight, yellow-black or nearly white with its prick ears and marvellous bushy tail distinguishing it from station dogs. Listening to the dingos howl at night was an unforgettable experience. So weird and mournful and definitely primaeval.

'I could stay here forever!' Nicky confided to Tait on one occasion and Tait had smiled and ruffled Nicky's hair indulgently, much as he did to Jamie.

'He's a fine boy,' he told Laura seriously, 'you've nothing to worry about there.'

And all of them (Philippa was naturally excepted) were so kind. There were Easter eggs and presents and Mrs Lambert's wonderful picnic lunches. Jamie basked in the older boy's company—Nicholas very kindly took him aside and showed him how to bat and bowl—but towards the end of the holiday Laura was feeling quite breathless with all the activity. It was go, go, go from first light. Even five-year-old Jamie was standing the pace better than she was.

'I'd like to go to school with Nicky,' Jamie announced, and in fact there were a few tears when it was time for Nicky's flight to the central Outback town where he would connect with the last leg of his trip.

'I want to thank you, sir, for the most fantastic holiday of my life.' Nicky shook Tait's hand with a great deal of enthusiasm.

'We enjoyed having you, Nick.' Tait looked at the boy with approval.

Nicky turned and hugged his sister to him with unselfconscious love, while behind them Jamie was

holding the best of his chocolate Easter eggs for
Nicholas to have on the plane.

'What a great little kid, you are!' Nicholas accepted
the present with much pleasure, never mentioning the
chocolate was melting. 'I mean it. A great little kid.'

Sitting in the jeep on the way back to the house
Laura brushed away a few tears while Jamie hugged
her in quick sympathy. 'You've still got me, Laura,' he
told her.

'He enjoyed it, didn't he?' Tait gave her one of his
beautiful, slow smiles.

'I know you won't listen . . .'

He waved the rest of it away.

'Thank you so much, Tait.' She looked at his strong
profile, the rugged, deeply indented chin. 'It was such
a time of discovery for him.'

'He's going to drop me a line,' Jamie said. 'I've
always longed to get a letter.'

From the elation of the long week-end Laura fell
into a slight melancholy. Reaction she supposed. The
house was very quiet without the two boys whirling
around and the McEwan family's friends. From what
she could discover the very attractive Christie
Clifford, who had kissed Tait very lingeringly while
she was waiting for her parents in the entrance hall,
was an old girlfriend.

'That was before that Kimberly Stewart, or was it
after?' Mrs Lambert had mused. 'There were so
many, you see.'

From the little Laura had seen of the very
enterprising Christie Clifford she was surprised
Christie had let him get away. She was a very
animated creature—in total contrast to the impeccable
Philippa who tended to sit like a figure in the
waxworks—in fact Laura had quite liked her. Aunt
Jessica had insisted she come to dinner on Easter
Saturday night but for the rest of the time Laura had
arranged that she took her meals with the boys. They
could never have waited for the family dinner hour for

a start. Miss Clifford with the big blue eyes had been startlingly friendly when one considered Philippa treated Laura as though she was an embarrassing ghost. Tait, too, had spent a lot of time lazily laughing at Christie and he certainly hadn't pulled away when Christie was thanking him so handsomely for having been such a marvellous host.

'She'll come again, mark my words!' Mrs Lambert told Laura, raising her eyes. 'Some of them have a very long habit of hankering after Mr Tait.'

Only Lorne Sutton welcomed the sudden solitude. During the entire Easter period he had given himself over to an orgy of work. Sketching me, Laura guessed. She had in fact managed two separate half hours while Jamie was having his cat naps but Lorne told her plainly he had planned on a lot longer sessions. He even looked the artist in soft, pale shirts and black jeans. Since he had arrived on the station he didn't bother much with having his hair trimmed so in consequence it was rather poetically long. But he did look different, more positive, as though he was slowly emerging from his deeply depressed state.

Aunt Jessica and Laura completed another two chapters, and just as Laura would have escaped Lorne now took to lying in wait for Laura telling her he could see his way to painting her portrait. It was almost as if she were some angel offering him salvation.

One late afternoon Jamie got tired of waiting for Laura. He pushed open the studio door and rushed blindly across to where Laura was rather draped in a gilded Louis chair.

'Leave that,' he shouted. 'You told me you'd be ready ages ago.'

'I am ready. I'll be ready soon.' Laura took one look at Lorne's black expression and caught Jamie's flailing hands.

'Do you know anything at all about knocking,' Lorne Sutton asked his son very tightly.

'I did knock,' Jamie fibbed. 'But Laura is my friend not yours.'

'You're a very rude little boy. You know that?'

'I'm not. I'm not. Tell him, Laura.'

'You can't shout, Jamie,' Laura told him quietly.

'Well, let's go.' He pulled on her hand.

'To suit you, a child!' Lorne Sutton threw down his paint brush.

'I am a little tired, Lorne,' Laura said in a gentle, apologetic way. 'Come, Jamie, tell your father you're sorry you rushed in.'

'I'm sorry, Daddy,' Jamie turned and gave his father the sweetest, most insincere smile. 'I'll go back now and knock.'

'It's no use at all!' Lorne declared temperamentally, stabbing a hand through his dark hair so it looked quite wild.

'Perhaps we can manage a little more time after dinner?' Laura tried to placate him if only for Jamie's sake.

'Oh yes.' He flushed a little and looked at her. 'You're such a sensitive person, Laura.'

'What's sensitive?' Jamie later asked. They were going for a short walk to the pink-lily lagoon.

'It means one is particularly aware of other people's feelings,' Laura explained. 'A sensitive person can read other people's moods and respond to them.'

'Daddy was angry with me.'

'Well darling,' Laura said fairly, 'you don't make a serious attempt to please him.'

'He doesn't try to please me. He didn't even buy me an Easter egg. I thought at first the big one was from him but of course it was Aunty Jessie.'

'Perhaps being here had something to do with it.' Laura tried to explain away Lorne's curious thoughtlessness. 'It's not as though he could pop out to the shops.'

'Then how come Uncle Tait flies everything in?'

'Your Uncle Tait, my darling, is a very rich man.'

'He could have got me an Easter egg,' Jamie said.

'I know it seems he wasn't thinking about you, Jamie, but it's not really his fault. Daddy is an artist.'

'You mean he's a bit dotty?'

'Dotty?' Laura looked down at the child in astonishment.

'Lamby said he was . . . a bit dotty.'

'To you?' Laura's eyes widened in dismay.

'Not to me,' Jamie was rather enjoying surprising Laura. 'She said to Scotty. Remember that time Daddy barked at Scotty?'

Barked was the wrong word. Lorne had been rather nasty.

'Daddy is a very intelligent man,' she told Jamie firmly. 'And you'll have to resist the habit of listening in to other people's conversations.'

'I don't try to,' Jamie looked up at her virtuously. 'You can hear Lamby everywhere.'

It was beautiful at the lagoon, with tree shadows falling across the emerald water intricately adorned with extraordinarily beautiful pink water lilies rising above a thick carpet of huge, green leaves. Not only were the lilies exquisite to look at, they were richly fragrant and the lily pads proved marvellous water beds for frogs. That afternoon Peter Delprat joined them there. Since Easter he had formed the habit of spending a good deal of his leisure time with Laura and Jamie, though even Jamie was aware of where his true interest lay.

'Hello there,' he now called to them, his brown hair smoothly combed and a dazzling smile on his face. He was a very attractive young man in an uncomplicated, let's-get-a-lot-of-fun-out-of-life kind of way and if Laura didn't exactly look on him as a kindred spirit she did enjoy his company in moderate doses. Unfortunately there was a certain tell-tale eagerness about him now and Laura thought vaguely she would have to invent a boyfriend back home. A complication she had never intended.

'I've been hearing all kinds of good things about you, Laura,' he cried enthusiastically and grabbed hold of a slender tree trunk to break his rapid descent down the bank.

'Oh?' She didn't really know what he was going to say.

'From Miss Jessica. I've just been speaking to her. She told me she didn't know what she would do without you.'

'We work very well together,' Laura replied.

'Hi, Jamie.' Peter's brown eyes dropped to the small boy.

'This is our place,' Jamie said.

'What's that supposed to mean?' Peter looked to Laura for an answer to his puzzlement. 'I could almost believe the little chap is jealous.'

'Yes I am,' Jamie said. 'I love Laura and when I grow up I'm going to marry her.'

'No, Jamie. Everything will be different then,' Laura explained a little ruefully.

'Yes I am.'

'Gosh!' Peter murmured after a long time. 'I suppose he's never quite got over . . .'

'No.' Laura interrupted firmly. 'We'll work it out.'

'I hope so.' Peter gave her a sidelong glance. 'You look lovely and cool.'

'Thank you.' The afternoon breeze caught at Laura's coiled hair, loosening a few silver-gilt strands. She was wearing an apple-green dress and her satin skin had taken on the palest gold sheen.

'We ought to go exploring again this weekend,' Peter said. 'No wonder your young brother loved it here. I thought he was going to refuse to go home.'

'He'll be back again,' Jamie pronounced, kicking some white pebbles into the water. No question his mood had changed.

'Well . . .' Peter laughed into the dappled sunlight. 'I thought we might take the horses into the hill country. Start out early Saturday morning.'

'No.' Jamie turned quickly to Laura. 'Oh-my-God is he sweet on you, Laura?'

It was a glorious imitation of Mrs Lambert and Laura thought not for the first time Mrs Lambert would have to be more careful in front of this very precocious five-year old.

'Jamie,' she said pleasantly, 'you must remember your manners.'

'I want to go for a swim.'

'Not in there, Jamie,' Peter said briskly. 'The lagoon is not for swimming.'

'You mean in the pool at home, don't you, Jamie?'

'Funny little tike, I've upset him,' Peter said wonderingly as Jamie ran away from them.

'He's been crying out for attention,' Laura said. 'He misses his mother dreadfully though he can't put it into words. I've become a sort of mother-substitute.'

'Ah yes, he wants to marry you when he grows up.'

'Lots of little boys say that.' Laura started to move forward a little anxiously.

'You sure know how to handle men and boys,' Peter told her admiringly. 'Your brother adores you and I'm fast losing my heart.'

'Don't do that, Peter.' Laura took time off to meet his nice brown eyes directly. 'You're just a bit lonely, that's all.'

'I don't think so,' Peter said. 'That Christie Whatsaname that was here at Easter, she was rather gorgeous but it wasn't at all the same.'

'I suppose not. She was clearly interested in Tait.'

'And what about you?' Peter enquired. 'Once or twice I've seen him look at you and I've wondered. You're a very beautiful girl, Laura, and that's not just a flowery compliment. There's a world of difference between you and say Christie. I suppose it's something deep in you beyond the shining eyes and blonde hair. Then you're so very quick.'

'I'll have to be if I'm going to catch Jamie,' Laura

suddenly cried. 'It's unbelievable isn't it? He's just a baby and he rushing away like a jealous suitor.'

'Sweetheart,' Peter said playfully, 'most of us start young.'

'I'll have to go after him . . .'

'Let's make it Saturday?' Peter urged her.

'I don't know.' Laura was already moving along the bank. 'I'll tell you tomorrow, Peter, if that's all right.' After all Peter had been a very pleasant companion over Easter and very nice to Nicky.

'Jamie,' she called out worriedly. 'Please stop, I'm getting a stitch in my side.'

In fact it seemed ridiculous but she had the feeling this had happened before. Perhaps Jamie meant it as a prank, because he ran faster and Laura wondered how those little legs could cover the distance so rapidly. It was getting on towards sundown and she knew the men would be returning to the compound. She had seen some of them crossing the watercourse straight ahead. They never rode fast. Usually they were only walking the horses.

'Jamie!' she burst out in half-conscious dread. 'Come back here.' She started to run hard now and Jamie looked back almost disbelievingly. Laura's hair was flying down her back and she looked upset.

'I'm coming,' he called tearfully. He had been rather enjoying himself up until then, but now he could see Laura's face properly and she looked very pink and serious. He knew well enough he was not behaving properly and now his legs weren't moving half so quickly. They had never walked this way before, but Laura was moving towards him in an all-time record run.

When Laura first caught sight of the men riding in fear hit her like a knife in the stomach. She almost staggered under its impact but righted herself quickly leaping over the mounds of tangled grass and fallen branches. Why, oh why, had she allowed Jamie to run off? Well, she hadn't allowed him, but she hadn't thought of the danger.

One minute the riders were a distance off then they were travelling in earnest, sustaining a cracking pace with Tait on his magnificent black Wellington riding up front. It was impossible to mistake rider or horse. He would never think to find anyone at the last waterhole at that hour and from a distance the lagoon was sheltered by a thick screen of trees and small blossoming shrubs.

It had to be done swiftly or it would never be done at all. Nothing mattered except that she get to Jamie. She had absolutely no fear for herself. This, more than anything, worked in her favour, lending every muscle in her slender body extra strength.

Tait riding ahead thought he would never forget the sight of Laura racing towards Jamie until his dying day. Jim, his foreman, saw her too, veering with Tait as he swerved the stallion violently away, heading off the other riders. Only Garvey went flying in, not even bothering to check why the Boss had swung sideways and the rest of them had followed his lead. There wasn't a thing to warn him—not even the girl's scream.

Laura had no thought of screaming. Her super abilities had taken over, the ones she had never really had to call on. Just beyond the periphery of her vision a stockman was bearing down on them and she knew if she didn't close on Jamie in under twenty seconds there would be one small child beneath the bay's powerful, flying legs.

Tait McEwan on the opposite bank had Garvey's bay sighted along his gun barrel. He could drop the animal at one shot but Laura was moving like some fleet-footed golden creature, snatching up Jamie and throwing them both backwards into the water.

Only then did Garvey pull his horse so it reared in violent protest, standing on its hind legs and all but unseating him. He saw the boy come up spluttering then splashing madly, but the lagoon had engulfed the girl completely.

'I'm coming, sonny!' Garvey called, his heart almost bursting, but before he had even quieted the bay and vaulted out of the saddle his granite-faced employer was ploughing through the heavy, lily-decked water with Jim the foreman, hammering down the slope after him.

Jamie, who had been taught to swim like most Australian children at a very early age, now put his head under water in a wonderfully brave attempt to find Laura, but his uncle caught him up powerfully and literally threw him through the air to his foreman's waiting arms.

'Laura!' Jamie shrieked and the terrible fright and anguish in his voice made Jim Foster hug him tightly and tell him over and over everything was going to be all right.

It took Tait McEwan barely seconds to find Laura with a few chops of his hands. He grasped her limp body and lifted her out of the water as though she weighed nothing, turning her in his arms so her head was hanging downwards.

Jamie began to scream and his uncle cracked out an order for the foreman to bring the child to the bank. Laura's breathing had turned to choking sounds and Tait lay her face downwards kneading the water out of her lungs. She was conscious but half-dazed and it seemed certain she had hit her head on some submerged obstacle, either a rock or a rotting log.

The men ringed them round, but not too close and the poor, unfortunate Garvey made several half-fearful attempts to excuse his slowed perceptions. 'I couldn't see what was coming, truly!'

No one listened.

'She'll be okay.' Jim Foster shook his head in relief, then with almost a military snap instructed one of the men to go for the jeep.

'Laura?' Jamie murmured, very gently touching one of Laura's outstretched hands.

Sick and dazed not withstanding she managed a faint smile.

'She's going to be all right, Uncle Tait?'

'Sure she is,' his uncle told him crisply. 'We'll get you both back to the house.'

Jamie in fact was so wobbly when he tried to stand up, he toppled down and his uncle picked him up and supported him against his chest. 'I saw you going to dive for Laura?'

'Oh, yes!'

'That's my boy.'

Jamie dropped his head against that hard chest and cried. 'It was my fault.'

'You can tell me all about it afterwards. I'm not angry Jamie. I know you understand that.'

Jamie nodded. 'Is Laura unconscious or something?'

Tait put the child into Jim Foster's hands. 'A bit concussed, Jamie. That means she's hit her head. We'll get her home now. You too.'

The hall was quiet and dark as they made their way across the deep verandah. 'We can't possibly upset Aunt Jessica,' Laura murmured a little sickly. She didn't realise how ashen she looked though she was much more alert now. 'Please, Tait.'

'Let's just sneak up the stairs,' Jamie whispered. He too feared he would be sick, and he wanted to tell Laura he was sorry.

'Do you think you can make it, Jamie?' his uncle asked.'

'Sure I can. You pick Laura up.'

'I'm all right,' Laura wavered. 'Really.' Tait was in fact supporting her but he had been very, very quiet.

No one appeared to be around but as they reached the curving stairway they heard chatter from the direction of the kitchen. 'Up we go,' Tait urged Jamie on, giving the child the tiniest nudge. 'You be the leader.'

'Right oh,' Jamie straightened up suddenly. 'Oh, Uncle Tait, has Laura fainted again.'

Laura, lying in Tait's arms had closed her eyes. 'No, darling, but the chandelier seems to be whirling madly.'

Of course she was very, very sick but the two of them looked after her, no fuss at all.

'You'll feel better now, Laura,' Jamie told her.

'Oh let me die.'

'I was sick like that when I fell off the swing,' Jamie said.

'Right, out of those wet clothes.'

For the first time Jamie really realised he was wet. 'I'm all right. Let's fix Laura first.'

'Leave me. Just leave me,' Laura wailed.

'It's not like Laura to be grumpy,' Jamie said.

'What the devil is the matter?' Philippa's voice crackled from behind them and Tait and Jamie swung around.

'Do you think you can go down to the kitchen, Philippa, and ask Mrs Lambert to come here?'

'But of course.' Instead of turning away Philippa moved further into Laura's bedroom. 'Am I to understand Jamie and Miss Kenmore have been taking a splash?'

'Yes we did,' Jamie looked at her with evident dislike.

'How delightful! Why, Miss Kenmore, you look dreadful! And look what you're doing to the silk coverlet.'

'Shove it, Philippa,' Jamie said shortly.

'Shove it?' Philippa's glossy head swivelled in shocked disapproval towards the child.

'Yes now, Philippa, if you don't mind,' Tait told her with a not uncharacteristic curtness. 'And we're keeping this quiet. We don't want to upset my aunt in any way.'

'Well . . . I see.' Philippa recoiled.

'I can get out of these wet clothes,' Laura whispered and started to elbow herself up. 'Jamie, please bring me my nightdress and robe. They're hanging just inside the wardrobe.'

Jamie moved very quickly. 'She's a real s—t, Philippa, isn't she?'

'My God, Jamie, your language!' Tait looked up swiftly, but his mouth twitched. 'You have Laura's things? Please bring them here.'

Mrs Lambert bustled in, seeming to take in the whole situation at a glance. 'If you fix up the little fella, Mr Tait, I'll attend to Miss Laura here.' For a solid woman she moved very quickly around the bed. 'Why you poor little girl, you're as white as a sheet.'

Tait, taking Jamie by the shoulder moved to the door. 'We'll watch her tonight and get Bob Grant in in the morning just to be sure. She took a fair blow on the head.'

'We'll be back, Laura,' Jamie called to her at the door.

Mrs Lambert asked no questions at all until she had Laura curled back in bed, her face shining clean and her hair caught back with a ribbon.

'Thank you, Mrs Lambert,' Laura said, 'you're a real mother.'

'With two daughters I know all about it.' Mrs Lambert arranged the soft lemon rug. 'You're looking a lot better now. More concentrated.'

'Yes, I was a bit dizzy for a while.' In fact she felt so weak she wanted to weep. 'It was my fault, you know.'

'What was, dear?' Mrs Lambert looked at her very kindly, as though nothing, nothing, could be Laura's fault.

'I allowed Jamie to run away from me . . .' her voice trailed off.

'You mean Jamie took off for some reason or another . . .'

'It was bad, Mrs Lambert. Really bad.' Laura hung her head. 'I don't think Tait will ever forgive me.'

'Dear girl, it wasn't your fault, whatever it was. That's the point!'

'The men were returning, not as they usually do, walking the horses almost, but galloping down on the creek. Jamie was in the way.'

'I heard that!' Philippa was again standing in the doorway her face frozen. 'Because of your criminal negligence you exposed that boy to danger?'

'Oh, don't, Miss Philippa,' Mrs Lambert said. 'Can't you see the poor girl is upset?'

'You don't belong here. You never have belonged here,' Philippa announced, the blue light in her pale eyes flaring.

Mrs Lambert stood between the bed and Philippa. 'Have you no kindness in you?'

'That's not for you to ask, Mrs Lambert,' Philippa returned icily. 'My great concern is for the family. I remind myself that I told Jessica not to hire her in the first place.'

'Do me a favour, Mrs Hill,' Laura shuddered, 'go away.'

'Not this time, my dear,' Philippa sneered. 'You're the only person in the world who calls me Mrs Hill.'

'I feel sure of that,' Laura said wryly. 'So unless you want me to call you something else, might I point out this is my room.'

'Of course it is!' Mrs Lambert seconded protectively.

'You wouldn't be so approving of Miss Kenmore here,' Philippa told her softly, 'if you knew more about her. Even the way she came here was all wrong.'

Mrs Lambert swung about and looked down at Laura. 'What's she talking about?'

'Miss Kenmore is a journalist.'

'Miss Kenmore is my secretary.' Aunt Jessica was outlined against the golden light from the corridor. 'What has happened, why is Laura in bed?'

'Why nothing more than an unplanned dip in the creek,' Mrs Lambert answered jovially.

'Laura, dear?' Aunt Jessica moved rather slowly towards the bed, obviously waiting on Laura's account. 'Why, Laura,' she said in dismay, 'you look very white?'

'You're not to worry Aunt Jessica,' Laura lifted

herself up with a great effort. 'I hit my head on a rock or something. I didn't see it.'

'Laura.' Aunt Jessica stopped, put out her hand and smoothed Laura's hair. 'How did this happen, my dear child?'

'I'll tell you how it happened, Aunt Jessica,' Philippa cried triumphantly.

'I forbid you, absolutely forbid you, to upset my lady.' Mrs Lambert looked grim.

Laura took Aunt Jessica's hand, her silvery-grey eyes enormous, almost swamping her white face. 'Jamie and I had a bit of a fright but we're quite all right. Tait simply had to drag me out of the lagoon and I'm deeply mortified because I was rather ill. There's nothing whatever for you to worry about.'

'What a blend of evasion and false anxiety,' Philippa laughed harshly. 'The fact of the matter is her stupidity nearly got Jamie killed.'

'Right,' Mrs Lambert turned on Philippa belligerently, 'you asked for it!'

'Lamby!' Aunt Jessica shook her soft grey head, but the hand in Laura's trembled.

'Yes, I should have been more careful, Aunt Jessica,' Laura said. 'I feel very, very badly that I allowed Jamie to run off, but I got to him in time.'

'You see?' Philippa cried as though her point was proved. 'I expect she was talking to that Peter Delprat. He's always hanging about.' Philippa's white skin was flushed with colour and she looked unusually alive. 'You never knew what you were going to start, Aunt Jessica, when you brought her here.'

'Nor, unhappily, how extreme you would become, Philippa,' Aunt Jessica pointed out. She was holding herself straightly but her eyes seemed to have sunk slightly in her head. 'I can't quite understand your animosity to Laura. It's always been there from the very first day. She has done nothing to you.'

'She's turned you against me, Aunt Jessica,' Philippa cried emotionally, 'think about *that*!'

'For the love of God!' Tait came back into the room, giving them all a hard, frowning stare. 'Is this the time for any further upset? It's better for Laura not to have any visitors at all.' His eyes looked away from Laura, who seemed to have shrunk, to his obviously upset aunt. 'Come along with me, Jess. I want a drink and you look like you need to sit down. All's well that ends well as they say. Laura's eyes are like saucers. She's been the real victim of this thing so I'll take it out on her another time.'

'I knew you'd understand, Tait,' Philippa said.

'Is Jamie all right?' Laura faintly asked.

'Fine.' His green eyes narrowed over her. 'He told me why he ran away. Jamie, being Jamie, nearly always does the wrong thing but when he does the right thing, like diving for you today, I'm very proud of him. Come along, Jess.' Tait took his aunt's arm very quickly and gently. 'Mrs Lambert will look after Laura and you and I will have a little talk.'

'I'd like a drink too, please, Tait,' Philippa crossed her thin arms across her breasts as though she were cold. 'I feel so awfully sorry for you all.'

'Have you ever in your born days seen such a troublemaker?' Mrs Lambert exclaimed later after they had gone. 'Talk about neurotic! She was quite different in the old days, but I reckon losing her husband unhinged her. He was the stability in her life. Of course she never loved him. Always loved Mr Tait. Only it's just a dream. I think he'd like to do something quite brutal and choke her. It was difficult to refuse to have her but gawd it's even more difficult persuading her to leave. Would you like a wee sip of water, dear?'

'Please, Mrs Lambert.' Laura lay back tremblingly. She had known in her bones he would blame her.

'I expect Jamie will try to run in here in a moment, so I'll just head him off.'

'No, let him come,' Laura begged. 'I don't want to see all his little fears and insecurities return. He may feel I'm cross with him. We have to sort it all out before he goes to sleep.'

'All right, dear,' Mrs Lambert said soothingly and held the glass of water. 'You might feel a little bit hungry later on.'

Tait returned alone when Jamie was curled up on Laura's bed.

'Hi, Uncle Tait,' Jamie said drowsily, 'would you like some barley sugar?'

'I'd rather have another Scotch.'

'Something for her headache, that's what Laura wants.' Jamie raised himself up on his elbow and stared into Laura's face. 'See, I told you Uncle Tait would come. I expect he'll fit on the other side.'

'How are you now, Laura?' Tait did in fact move to the opposite side of the bed.

'Much better,' she answered truthfully. 'Jamie is a tonic.'

'God knows what he'll be like when he's my age.'

'Like you,' she smiled.

'My dear Laura I wasn't nearly so precocious.'

'So you say.' She winced slightly as she turned her head.

'Show me.'

'It's as big as an Easter egg,' Jamie said. 'When I touched it Laura groaned.'

'It is a bump,' Tait conceded, his fingers exploring Laura's scalp with extreme gentleness. 'As it happens, I have a couple of pain killers with me.'

'Great!' Unless she was mistaken he was pale beneath the deep tan. 'I feel very badly about this afternoon.'

'Insofar as I can make out you were distracted by young Delprat?' He poured water into a glass, set it down, and extracted two white tablets from his breast pocket.

'I think Peter is really in love with Laura,' Jamie pronounced.

'I told you he was a scary kid.' Tait slipped an arm behind Laura's back.

'Well we can't say he gets his ideas from the television. Peter was only being friendly, that's all.' Laura put the two tablets in her mouth and swallowed them with plenty of water. 'Ugh!'

Jamie laughed delightedly. 'Do they taste awful, Laura?'

She nodded. 'I believe I should have asked what they were.'

'Trust me,' Tait urged. 'I guess we're all in shock.' He turned his head and looked away across the room with mock casualness. 'No noise. No sound at all. Everything quiet. Another day. Consider how I felt.'

'We'll never go there again,' Jamie said. 'Never!'

'You,' Tait pointed to him very hard, 'know much better than Laura does that's a crossing. Furthermore, if Laura orders you to stop, you stop!'

'Yes, Uncle Tait.' Jamie covered his eyes with his fists.

'Please don't be hard on him, Tait,' Laura pleaded. 'He's so little!'

'Little my foot! He's a tiger.'

It was well into the evening when Aunt Jessica called back, bringing with her Lorne's fervent wish she was feeling much better.

'I must say he sounded sincerely upset,' Aunt Jessica confided. 'We simply told him you had fallen and hit your head. Sometimes Jamie is a little demon but we felt he had had enough punishment for one day. Children will run away and neither of you were to realise the risk. Normally the men never approach at a gallop, only this evening they did. It really is a place to avoid.'

'I will, Aunt Jessica,' Laura said and almost crossed herself.

'What was in those tablets Tait gave you?' Aunt Jessica leaned closer staring into Laura's luminous eyes.

'I don't know but I feel better. Perhaps a little groggy.' She smoothed back a silky strand of her hair. 'I'm glad you're not angry with me.'

'What do you mean, angry?' Aunt Jessica gently chided her. 'Tait tells me you were very brave and so when it came to it was our little Jamie. God was good.'

She must have fallen off to sleep and when she awoke again Tait was standing at the foot of the bed staring at her with taut concentration.

'Tait?' She lifted her head a little vaguely.

'How are you now?' The strange intensity of his expression smoothed out to a softer concern.

'Oh, better I think. I've been asleep for ages and ages.'

'Not so long.' He glanced at his watch. 'Mrs Lambert brought you up a supper tray but she didn't have the heart to wake you. How's the head?'

She sat up slightly, adjusting the tiny puffed sleeve of her nightdress. 'Alas, still there.' She felt a spasm of pain.

'You might need some more help to sleep.'

'No, I don't think so. I don't like taking tablets.'

'Neither do I but this time we'll defer to a doctor's judgment. If you're not feeling a lot better in the morning he'll come and see you.'

'I'm sure I'll be fine.' She didn't know how young she looked with her blonde hair in a ribbon and her skin with a child's gloss. 'You were looking at me so strangely when I woke up.'

'I'm sure I was,' he agreed dryly and came to the side of the bed. 'I'm sure of late my expression has been undergoing lots of changes.'

'I don't think I could bear it if you decided to dislike me.' She couldn't seem to take her eyes off him, the whole vivid presence, so darkly, ruggedly handsome in the soft, silken opulence of this lovely, feminine bedroom.

'Please stop talking like an idiot.' He sat down on the side of the bed and she moved a little to accommodate him.

'Then what did that expression mean?'

His eyes were very clear and green in the muted,

golden light. 'And I thought you were smart enough to interpret my every glance?'

'No way!' She gave a jagged little sigh. 'As I recall you said you were going to speak to me at another time.'

'I don't think I need to now.' He lifted one of his hands and put a finger beneath her chin. 'You didn't care a thing for yourself, did you, this afternoon?'

'All I kept seeing was Jamie running beneath a horse's hooves.' She must have been still slightly drugged because involuntarily she turned her cheek along his hand.

'You will please not incite me tonight,' he told her, almost violently.

'T-Tait?' She was so shocked she stuttered, then as if coming out of a dream she saw the naked desire on his face and the cat-like glitter of his eyes. She wanted to tell him how much she loved him but she was afraid for so many reasons.

'Poor little Laura,' he said mockingly, 'weighed down with so many considerations.'

'I'll try to master them,' she managed to say calmly.

'You mean you're terrified of loving me,' he contradicted her flatly.

'What if I am?' Her luminous eyes flashed in a kind of despair. 'There doesn't seem much point in it, does there? I have to go home eventually and you belong out here. A king in his castle. Besides, you seem to prefer a bachelor's life.'

'I could give it up tomorrow,' he told her with very grand complacency. His finger moved down her chin and his hand enclosed her slim throat. 'You look very vulnerable tonight, Laura. Very young and fragile with your natural resilience diminished. Sometimes I forget how very delicate you are. How much stronger your spirit is than your body. It was a tremendous shock to me this afternoon seeing you in so much danger, or near danger. I could have stopped it but you weren't to know that. I think I lived through ten life times in seconds then my reaction, I think, was a little irrational. I wanted to beat you, but the sight of you, the feel of you cancelled that out irrevocably. You're really just a slip of a girl, a golden creature to cherish.'

'I suppose it might be wonderful,' she gave him the shadow of her smile, 'but I'd still like to offer plenty of opinions and do my own thing.'

'All the best women do.' His green glance moved lingeringly over her satin-smooth skin. 'Do you think if I kissed you it would worsen your headache or cure it?'

He kept it light; so did she. 'We won't know until you try.'

'I can't stay on, of course.'

'No.' Beneath the banter, myriad sensations were stirring, ready to surge if one dared. He was applying no pressure at all to her yet somehow her body was arching towards him and her quivering mouth unknown to her was framing itself to meet his.

'Laura,' he repeated, 'Laura.' It wasn't melting, but almost admonishing. He laughed abruptly and pulled the ivory ribbon that tied her hair. It swirled in a heavy mass and his green eyes darkened and the set of his dominant features almost hardened. 'I'll be very, very careful.' He cupped her head in his hands and caught up her parted lips with his own, an enforced kind of gentleness that nevertheless had a white-hot intensity.

She didn't dare to breathe, but after a moment she twisted to get nearer him and all at once he lifted her, drawing her backwards into the curve of his arms and his shoulder. 'Oh, God!' he said softly, as though he should have known neither of them would be able to hold back.

Laura let go of everything . . . every last restraint, every last inhibition. His mastery of her was absolute. It was impossible to deny what she felt for him. She could only do that in the waking hours with a lot of talk. He had only to touch her to discover the real truth. Just touch her to disturb and put to flight all the cover-ups she felt necessary for pride and self-protection. She wasn't protecting herself now. She was allowing him to crush her to him in immeasurable surrender.

Yet curiously her total yielding imposed on him a greater restraint. The tension in him was tantalising; the deliberate holding-back.

'Oh Tait, I want you so badly.' Did she say that? Put it foolishly into words. But there was silence only for their quickened breathing.

Then suddenly he lifted his head and she opened her eyes and looked up into his face.

'This is madness, little one,' he said.

'Is it?' Her eyes were enormous and bemused.

'You don't remember you hit your head rather badly?'

She rested back against his arm. 'I only remember kissing you. Apart from that, nothing.'

'Well as—as your—what am I, for God's sake?'

'I look on you as—as . . .' The lover I've waited for all my life, she thought ardently.

'I think you'd better go back to bed,' he decided briskly. 'With any luck we might hit on the truth at the same time.'

CHAPTER NINE

To please everyone Laura did little or nothing the next day and Jamie decided he had earned a rest as well. They sat in the brilliant sunshine and Jamie swam in the pool, but Laura felt as though all her strength had temporarily drained away. She was thinner, she thought. Thinner, in a day? But it certainly seemed like it and her eyes were larger than usual. Lakes.

Peter came to tell her he found himself shocked such a drama had happened almost under his nose. He had moved away quickly, intending to return to the station office but had he troubled to look back he would have seen young Jamie making such incredible headway.

'Not exactly the usual kind of little chap, is he?'

'I don't suppose he could be,' Laura replied. 'McEwan blood on one side and Lorne for a father.'

'Now there's a strange bloke!' Peter uttered. 'I know it must have been agonising losing his wife but he doesn't seem to give a hang about Jamie. How on earth could that little fellow survive without the McEwans? For that matter a lot of people seem to lean pretty heavily on Tait.' Peter, sitting on the grass, looked up at Laura carefully. She was resting on a recliner beneath a heavily fringed blue-and-white umbrella. 'Was there some kind of love affair between Tait and Philippa Winston-Hill? Gosh, isn't that a mouthful?'

'I just call her Mrs Hill,' Laura murmured.

'You would. You could get away with anything,' Peter said admiringly and leaned forward to swing her fingers. 'You look beautiful with your hair blowing like that.'

'It feels good.' She opened her eyes momentarily. 'Is Jamie all right?'

'Good as gold.' Peter glanced nonchalantly towards the huge, inground pool. 'He's a bloody handsome little kid. Like Tait, wouldn't you say? Nothing like the father at all.'

'No, he's a McEwan,' Laura agreed, hoping Peter would forget about Philippa.

'I suppose that Philippa is a very good-looking creature too but I find her horrible. She's so cold.'

'With us, dear boy.'

'You mean she's transformed around Tait? Tell me about it. I thought that Christie was mad for him?'

'He is terribly attractive.' Laura kept her voice light.

'Attractive? Hell, that doesn't say it. Even yours truly has been called attractive. No, Tait is dynamic. I suppose he'd have to be to keep all this going. Always on the move yet that fabulous energy apparently never drains away. And the station is only part of his holdings. He's into everything, believe me.'

'Diversifying, that's the word you want.'

'I wonder what it's like being incredibly rich?'

'Difficult from all accounts.'

'I wouldn't mind it,' Peter said. 'Some are very fortunate, aren't they? Fancy growing up here. I mean the homestead is just a palace! He wouldn't know how ordinary people lived at all.'

'I think they say that about Prince Charles, don't they, yet he moves very easily among the rest of us. I suppose it's all a matter of training. Many rich and powerful people take duty and responsibility very seriously. They're aware of their moral obligations.'

'I suppose.' Peter looked as though he thought just as many were prepared to trample on their lesser brothers. 'Anyway Tait is a good bloke. It would be an unspeakable crime out here to suggest anything else and the Aboriginals seem to know and trust him. They've got a name for him. What is it?'

'Byamee, something like that. I think it means Great Spirit, or White Father, or something.'

'Are you in love with him, Laura?' Peter abruptly asked.

'What's this?' She turned her head swiftly, feigning amazement.

'You seem to look at each other all the time. Others mightn't understand what all the banter means but I think I do. You're very wrapped up in him.'

'But of course! He's a very admirable man.'

'There you go again!' Peter said wryly. 'I don't mind if you've fallen in love with him. I can understand it, but you'd better not forget you have an enemy in Philippa. She'd make you suffer if she could. There's something about her, something that's quite odd. I know Miss Jessica has had enough of her. Nothing she has told me—she would never say anything—but I sense her unease. In the beginning she was supposed to come for a few weeks but it has run on into months. In the end, I suppose, Tait is bound to kick her out. He might have cared about her at one time but anyone with half an eye could see it's over.'

'I don't suppose unhappy people see too clearly,' Laura said. 'And some when they fall in love, it's like a religion. As soon as I saw Philippa I thought she had the look of a crazy zealot.'

'You have a way with words,' Peter laughed.

Peter was still with her when Tait returned unexpectedly for lunch.

'Hi, there!'

Laura expected it to come out dry and sarcastic but it didn't. Only his eyes looked mocking.

'Uncle Tait, Uncle Tait,' Jamie cried. 'Watch me dive.'

'Okay.' Tait waved his hand. 'How are you feeling, Laura?'

'Enjoying being quiet.'

'Well, I'll cut along,' Peter looked faintly embarras-

sed. 'Is there anything in particular, Tait, you want
me to do?'

'You could ride out with us this afternoon. We're
working the Seven-Mile.'

'Oh, great!' Peter's dark golden face lit up. 'Do you
think if I kept at it I could learn to manage a station?'

'Yes, if you're serious.'

'I love the life.'

'You haven't seen the bad times.'

'No—it must be terrible.'

'Don't encourage that boy,' Tait said when Peter
had gone.

'Oh God, as if I would.'

'I thought beautiful girls quite enjoyed it?'

'Do you think I'm encouraging you?'

'Of course you are.' His green eyes glinted. 'But I'm
well over the impressionable age. It's even possible
you're a little at my mercy.'

'Did you see that, Uncle Tait?' Jamie called.

'I did but your arms aren't right. I'll show you
tonight.'

'I can show him,' Laura said.

'Don't worry today.' He flickered a glance over her
face and shadowed eyes. 'Take my advice and relax.'

'Sure, Boss. Isn't that what the men say?'

'I don't expect it from you.'

She looked up at him standing there, very tall and
lean, with his wide-brimmed Stetson tilted at a rakish
angle on his dark, curling head. 'What do you expect,
Tait?'

'From you?'

Something in his expression made her heart lurch.
'Yes.'

'The truth. Nothing else.'

'Is that something I have to unravel?'

'I'm not going to do it for you.'

She puzzled over that for the rest of the afternoon.

A fortnight came and went and now they were more

than half way through Aunt Jessica's book. Laura read
it in bed each night and often she took the old diaries
with her as well. Her interest was so great and she had
done so much research Aunt Jessica told her she was
almost as much an authority on this pioneering family
as Aunt Jessica was herself.

Philippa stayed on, filling her days and staring right
through Laura at night, but Lorne had become much
more communicative. Laura sat for him on several
occasions and he must have liked his preliminary
sketches for it seemed he had launched into oils on a
canvas the size of which made her gasp.

'You're my favourite person at the moment, Laura,'
he told her and Laura began to pray this moment
would pass. Surely his own little son should be his
favourite person on earth, yet Lorne seemed to be
completely without a paternal feeling. Everyone on the
station had noticed it and repeated quietly among
themselves what Mrs Lambert had been heard to
exclaim openly: 'Miss Anne should never have
married him!'

Because it was so natural to her, Laura had taken to
jotting down sketches of the various people on the
station who interested her. Just as Lorne captured
likenesses on paper or canvas, Laura did it with words.
She wrote about Tait. Of course, Tait. Aunt Jessica,
marvellous warm studies that brought a well-loved
author to life. Lorne, who emerged a rather weak
character but with a terrible, natural charm. She did
not write about Philippa, although she had never met
anyone remotely like Philippa before. She wrote about
Scotty and several of the stockman, all superb
horsemen.

She put down the story of poor Charlie, who had
been rescued at death's door by the wiles of Father
O'Neill from the mission. Father O'Neill had crept up
behind Mindji, the old sorcerer, and snipped off a lock
of his hair which Mindji took to mean Father O'Neill
intended to practise 'plenty magic' against him.

Mindji had expected some retaliation against Jacky as Charlie's condition worsened, but apparently he had never considered potent magic might be worked on him. Versions differed, but all were in agreement Father O'Neill was a particularly powerful man. Charlie recovered and so did Mindji, from a foot injury the white man would have thought had less to do with magic than a bullock stepping on it. The key was the powers of persuasion and Father O'Neill took the prize, though he roared about it afterwards over one of Mrs Lambert's wonderful dinners washed down with fine wine. Laura found herself chuckling as she wrote about it afterwards.

In fact, she was missing her writing. Later on, perhaps, when she had experienced more, she might attempt a novel. She had a natural facility for writing and she did enjoy it so. It was a pity in a way the family were so against giving interviews, she knew many readers all over the country would enjoy reading about them. All she had done on Lorne would have to be dressed up. It wasn't a cruel study (Laura didn't have a cruel bone in her body) but it was penetratingly true. Lorne Sutton was the complete egotist, given over entirely to his own ambitions and feelings. His wife, Anne, could not have had an easy time with him and perhaps, who knows, she turned to another man for comfort. However innocently or briefly. A woman found it hard to live without understanding and there couldn't have been a lot of that feeling in the marriage. Lorne was a pretty shallow person really and that could explain why his work, though dazzling in its technical expertise, lacked true greatness. There had to be the heart behind the hand.

Rather sadly Laura put her large exercise book away. Maybe at some time in the future Lorne could come to feel for somebody else. Laura had the appalling notion if the family expressed the desire to take over the rearing of Jamie, Lorne might accede with relief. Certainly he didn't intend Jamie to live with him once he returned to normal life. Jamie was too much of a handful; too forthright and demanding. Jamie even at five made his presence felt. Lorne didn't want that. He had to be entirely free, otherwise life for an artist made no sense at all. So Laura committed her intimate thoughts to paper, working out personalities and allowing her perceptions to grow and grow. Goodness, she needed to write. Certainly Aunt Jessica would understand that. She even thought pleasurably of trying her hand at a romance-thriller. Surely being a writer had to be one of the most satisfying jobs there was? It had to be a job. She needed money.

Towards the end of the month there were a good many interruptions. Tait had two important American buyers staying on the property during the very time Mrs Lambert trod on one of Jamie's toys, went skidding into a straight-backed Victorian chair which went down under her weight and in fact hit her in the eye as she fell. It was a spectacular accident, sending the housegirls into shrieks of stifled mirth and Laura racing anxiously to Mrs Lambert's aid. The upshot, one black eye and a wrenched ankle, which on such a substantial lady could well have been broken.

'Go and get help, Jamie,' Laura had swiftly ordered, and Jamie had returned with four stock boys who found it quite a task transporting Mrs Lambert to her room.

'Whatever shall we do?' Aunt Jessica asked, dumbfounded. She had never considered it odd that she had never learnt to cook, but Laura had wasted no time finding out. Her mother had been a marvellous cook and even then she had sent Laura along to an excellent cooking school to acquire what she considered the essential skills. The days of having servants were over, except for the very rich, so Laura's offer to help couldn't have come at a better time.

'Not exactly what we had in mind,' Philippa commented scathingly, then had to lapse into furious silence as Laura managed very well. Mrs Lambert from her bed wrote long lists of what she could do and how to roster the domestic tasks which Laura read and nodded over but eventually pressed on with her own menus and organisation. She even managed to accelerate Lucy and Leila, the two little housegirls' almost snail-like progress, jogging them just short of the point where they fell into the sulks. In fact Laura felt a warm glow of pride in her own expertise, but Tait appeared to accept it as though it was fairly obvious Laura could do anything if she tried.

'I had no idea you were so domesticated, my dear!' Aunt Jessica cried. 'Fancy you acquired your degree and still found the time to become such a spectacular cook. We're terribly impressed.'

Laura had to fight back her laughter. Indeed sometimes she had the peculiar feeling that at Eagle's Ridge she had somehow taken a step back in time, to slower, more luxurious times when a lot of people died from overwork and those on top lived a life of magical ease. Still if it was true in the very early pioneering days the McEwans as a family had suffered greatly, they moved into the twentieth century splendidly.

'You're a big hit, Laura,' Jamie told her.

'Did you hear someone say that?' she asked him.

'Yes.' Jamie spent a lot of his time listening in to the adults. Too much time Laura feared. She had come to love him, delighting in his extraordinary barrage of chatter, but she felt very sorry for him as well. Jamie who had lost his mother couldn't go to his father with his little jokes. The relationship was observed but Laura was given to wondering over and over why Lorne showed little sign of pride in his handsome and fearless little son. Maybe he lacked a paternal feeling altogether? It seemed incredible and as Laura began to feel, a calamity for Jamie. She had never really cared for Lorne Sutton from their first meeting and these days she wanted to kick him for his virtual abandonment of his little son. He didn't even seem to realise Jamie almost picked a fight with his father just to gain some attention. Jamie would never take to being ignored.

'You really love that boy, don't you?' Mrs Lambert asked her quite emotionally. Enforced inactivity was driving her towards melancholia.

'Of course I love him,' Laura responded. 'In fact I'm going to suffer when I have to leave.'

On the fourth day the patient was allowed up and Jamie went down with a passing fever that necessitated Laura's nursing him, because he seemed too distressed for anyone else.

'Stay with me Laura,' he cried fretfully whenever she looked like she was about to move off.

'Of course I'll stay with you!'

Aunt Jessica's book was abandoned. 'We'll get back to it next week, dear,' she told Laura a little helplessly. 'I begin to yearn for the house to ourselves.'

What Aunt Jessica really meant was she hoped Philippa would go home, or as Philippa's parents had semi-disassociated themselves from their difficult daughter, Philippa would find a place of her own.

'She's certainly not short of cash,' Aunt Jessica confided to Laura very quietly. 'I'm rather sorry for the poor girl but surely she must now begin to lead her own life?'

It was a wail from the heart, for Philippa was causing some embarrassment with her obvious antipathy to Laura. If she spoke to Laura at all she spoke very sharply, when it would have been much better in every way to at least observe the civilities.

Perhaps Jamie couldn't have put it a better way, though Laura took it upon herself to cure him of sprinkling his conversation with the kind of exclamations much in vogue when the horses or cattle were playing up. Such words, almost pleasantries among the stockmen, were fatal at the dinner table and staggering from a flower-eyed five-year old.

Lorne Sutton for his part was kept busy on his portrait of Laura.

'I hope he's going to let us see it,' Jamie confided to Laura as though there wasn't much chance.

'Could I see it, Lorne?' Laura found herself asking one morning on impulse.

'Certainly, my dear,' Lorne told her with a glint of weary amusement. 'When I'm ready.'

'When Daddy's ready,' Laura passed on.

Of course Philippa pronounced herself shocked such an eminent artist would wish to paint anyone with so little . . . living in her face.

'What about the celebrated Renoirs?' Tait drawled. 'It's a terribly dull artist who hasn't painted a beautiful girl. And Laura is beautiful. There's no doubt about that.'

Such championing hit Philippa severely. She only just managed to wait until she found Laura alone. 'Well, you've fixed yourself up very nicely here, haven't you?' she accused Laura. 'Trying to ingratiate yourself at every turn.'

Laura tried to shrug it off. 'It might help if you tried to ingratiate yourself a little,' she suggested. 'The family like me and I would have thought that you as their guest would pretend a little liking, or if that proved too much remember to be civil.'

'My God, you're too much,' Philippa exclaimed. 'I think you're becoming very muddled about where you really stand. I am the one who is almost family. You are a paid employee and quite an opportunist as it happens.'

Laura rose abruptly and slammed her book shut. 'Lay off, Philippa,' she said briskly. 'At least I'm earning my keep.'

The shock of it almost threw Philippa back against the cedar double-doors. 'I'll make you sorry for that!' The blue, blazing eyes were naked with hate, the white skin pulled so taut one could almost see the skull beneath.

'You're not well, don't you see?' Laura managed more moderately, appalled at the other woman's high-strung tension. 'You don't bother to eat and this in a sense must threaten your mental well-being. Your attitude to me is one of the most intense bitterness . . .'

'I hate you,' Philippa flatly interrupted.

'In God's name, why?' Laura asked very seriously, looking directly into Philippa's strange light eyes. 'What harm have I done you? You don't even know me.'

'I can't stand to have you here,' Philippa acknowledged. 'I knew the moment I laid eyes on you you would threaten my life.'

'But that's insane!' Laura was literally transfixed.

'Is it?' Philippa's red mouth worked. 'It only takes seconds for a woman's intuition to be set in motion.' Her voice was full of anger and pain. 'I'm quite aware that you're in love with Tait just as I was aware from the beginning that he was attracted to you. You're quite a frightening person.'

'Me?' Laura gave a profoundly disturbed sigh. 'I couldn't frighten anyone if I tried.'

'Alas, you frighten me,' Philippa said oddly. 'You're not the only beautiful girl who has held Tait's attention but never for long. You have a great deal more than looks.'

'Well thank you for that,' Laura said wryly.

'Women like you acquire power over a man. They keep seeing more.'

'And you think if I weren't here Tait would ask you to marry him?' Laura asked with an involuntary lurch of pity.

'That's exactly what I think,' Philippa said.

'I'm sorry. Very sorry.' Laura drew in her breath. 'I think I know what agony it must be loving a man who never makes a move, but after a while I'd have to consider what I was doing with my own life. I know you're going to hate me even more for saying it, but I'm sure Tait isn't in love with you.'

'Don't be too sure of that,' Philippa said tonelessly. 'If he didn't care for me, how could he possibly take me in?'

'In friendship?' Laura suggested anxiously. 'He took his brother-in-law in in his grief. We're told on every hand what a fine man Tait is, caring and generous. It must be terrible to be deluded by romantic dreams.'

Philippa's white face flushed scarlet. 'Deluded is what I am not!' she cried violently. 'I've always wanted Tait and what's more I'm going to get him.'

The queer violence of Philippa's outburst subdued Laura for the rest of the day. Indeed, she found it difficult to concentrate her mind.

'Why don't you go out for a ride?' Aunt Jessica suggested. 'You've been working jolly hard.'

'Don't go without me,' Jamie pleaded, almost tearful, but Aunt Jessica came to Laura's rescue. 'I thought you might like to play with grandfather's soldiers.'

'Truly, Aunty Jessie?' Jamie's eyes went round with astonishment.

'I don't see why not. You're a very careful child and you appreciate that they're very old and quite valuable. What say we stage a battle?'

Laura slipped out.

One of the boys saddled up Lady, a quiet chestnut, for her, and Laura rode out. She had become much stronger and more confident in the saddle and she only intended going some little distance in the direction of Arrilka.

Philippa's enmity was upsetting her more and more each day. It wasn't until then that she realised how hard she had worked at ignoring it. Philippa behaved as though she were in the grip of a fantasy and it was completely useless to try and talk common sense. She had become programmed to love Tait—no, not love, more an obsession. Tait may or may not have cared for Philippa at one stage but Laura was certain his feelings had turned to part-impatience, part-support. Laura believed he now thought of Philippa as a burden, a burden that might go away of her own accord before he had to tell her. Of course the

connection was long and strong and as she rode Laura
began to question her own evaluation of the situation.

Didn't she believe, really believe that Tait was just a
little in love with her? Certainly she excited powerful
feelings in him but she could not forget men in Tait's
position often married heiresses of their own world.
Basically if she went away would Tait forget her? It
was the same old dilemma generally settled with
daisies. He loves me—he loves me not. In actuality
Tait could be indulging a mutual strong attraction
which had nothing to do with taking on a life's mate.
One thing for certain he wouldn't consider anyone so
extraordinarily difficult and intense as Philippa.

Laura had been riding quite a while before she
decided to round back. In the golden bliss of late
afternoon some of her anxieties were dissipated but
just as many remained. Birds fluttered in the acacias
and as the sun sloped to the west deep shadows ran
down the corridors of deep scrub. This was a rather
lonely part of the run but wonderfully interesting for
its undisturbed state. There were stone altars of the
Aborigines of long ago with sacred and secret
hieroglyphics cut into the slabs of rock. She
dismounted once to examine a curious ring of
cylindrical greyish-white stones and as she trod the
thick grass to the site a kangaroo half-buried in cane
grass suddenly bounded towards her while the birds
flew shrieking into the higher branches of the white-
boled limewoods.

'Go way . . . way!' Laura yelled and the kangaroo
thoroughly startled, very kindly obeyed her. It
thumped away vigorously, somehow inspiring Laura's
chestnut to take to her heels.

'Damn!' Laura swung around in consternation as
the chestnut galloped at least two hundred yards off,
displaying a swift stride Laura had been unable to
encourage.

'Come back!' She tried whistling but the chestnut
had galloped into a thicket of overhanging trees and

soon it was apparent it was going to run right on back to the compound.

'Dear God!' Laura whispered to herself, taking stock of her surroundings. The beautiful afternoon now seemed ominously quiet. Even the ever-present flocks of birds were still. At least there were no dangerous animals in the Outback. Snakes, of course. Huge, six-foot lizards, wild dogs, wild pigs, wild camels. Only a week before two of the stockmen had brought a half-grown wild camel in. The massive herds of cattle were fanned out across the plains country but there were rogues and some wild bull called Mudji about. One wouldn't need to run into a wild bull on foot, especially in the aloneness of the bush. All of a sudden she felt terribly small, like a junior explorer in a trackless waste. She had no idea she had come so far, though as soon as she reached that rise she would be in sight of the homestead complex. She checked her watch—5.15. The pure, silvery sweet notes of some bird floated down to her from a magnificent ghost gum. It called confidence and challenge. It would be quite a hike but she should be back at the homestead before dark. She didn't hold out much hope for herself after that. The transition from radiant light to pitch black was amazing. But then she had the stars. The tip of the Southern Cross hung directly over the house.

Laura walked on, stooping now and then to add to her beautiful collection of wild flowers. The scent of the tiny native violets was delightful but she wasn't on a cross-country ramble, she had to get back. Lady returning riderless would raise the alarm, but she hoped and prayed Aunt Jessica and Jamie wouldn't become distressed. Thinking this Laura broke into a constant jog. Drat Lady! She had acted like the quietest nag imaginable then took off like a racehorse confronted by a hostile beast. Out here horses and range-bred horses roamed together. She would have to give Lady a good talking-to.

The sunset display was tremendous; crimson and gold and thousands of wings. The birds came from everywhere, huge congregations homing in to water. The vibration of their countless wings was almost a muted thunder. She would always associate the Outback with birds. Birds and heart-stopping distances. She slowed a little to avoid a threatening stitch in her side. In her final year at school she had won the annual cross-country run and she was rather pleased she had kept herself in good condition. Everyone was into aerobics at home and she reminded herself to write to a couple of her girlfriends.

There was a brief period when she started to feel a little agitated, then she got her second wind. In fact she was jogging on strongly when the cloud of red dust in the distance cleared to a speeding jeep.

'My hero!' Laura yelled, slowing to a complete stand-still. Didn't she know it all along? She just had to hang in there and help would arrive.

Help wore a granite face.

'Hi, there!' she called a little weakly as Tait braked to a halt beside her.

He didn't even answer but unwound all six-feet-three of himself and almost leapt from the jeep.

'Lady bolted,' she explained. Heavens she thought he ought to be happy now not raring to give her a good shaking.

'Don't you ever—ever—ride off again.' He did grip her by the shoulders, staring down at her with darrk hostility and a flash of green eyes.'

'But I go for a ride all the time.'

'Not anywhere as far as this,' he bit off tersely.

'Well I'm sorry,' she said in sudden irritation. 'I'm not Jamie, you know, five-years old.'

He gave a nearly savage laugh. 'My dear girl if you were you'd have bother sitting down for at least a month. Do you know just what a fright it gave us?'

'Aunt Jessica?' Laura stared up at him her eyes full of dismay.

'No, me, you little fool.' His expression was very hard and beneath his dark tan she could discern a faint pallor. 'I hadn't reckoned on seeing that chestnut galloping in riderless.'

'Oh, I'm sorry, Tait.' She dipped her head.

'*Damn* you, Laura!' He pulled her to him violently.

'Don't you think you're over-reacting?' Instantly she was as angry as he was, feeling the heat in him, the queer rage that was of course a pent-up frustration.

'I was utterly prepared to find you . . . dead.'

She couldn't speak, instead her beautiful eyes filled with tears and he groaned in agony and crushed her to him, forcing her head back to kiss her mouth.

The world spun. He loved her. He had to love her or how else could he hold her with this completeness of possession? They remained there for moments while she didn't even fight his overpowering grip. His mouth was infinitely masterful, not gentle at all, so slowly she began to think she might crumple. Perhaps it was the arch of her neck or the tumultuous excitement that was threatening her consciousness.

'Tait?' As a plea it sounded extraordinarily weak.

'God, just allow me to hold you.'

'All right, but it's painful.'

'Hell!' He slackened his iron grip and his mouth moved to her cheek, her ear, the lovely line of her jaw. 'I don't want to face a day like this again.'

'And all because Lady bolted.' Her voice was tender.

'She could have thrown you.' There was a faint quiver in his strong arms. 'You've improved immensely but you're a long way from being an experienced rider. Why ever did you come so far and in this direction? Surely you know this is the loneliest part of the run?'

'And so interesting.' Rather tentatively she touched a finger to the deep cleft in his chin. 'I was all right, you know. I would have made it back.'

'Yes.' He stared away from her, over her blonde

head. He was fast regaining his composure but the pallor was still there. 'I never thought I would be over-protective or fuss over a woman but sometimes you have me just—mad!'

'You must love me then. Do you?'

'I think you'd make a handful of a wife.'

'You're unable to tell me?' she asked, very sadly.

'I think it's as plain as it could be you mean an awful lot to me.' So now he was back to mockery as though the force of feeling was something too highly charged and unusual. 'Yes, I love you, Laura,' he said almost coolly as she swung away. 'I never rattle on about love.'

'Why, are you frightened of it?' She flung up her chin.

'Don't you think it's rather frightening?' he challenged her. 'I could have let the whole station go to hell chasing after you.'

'Ah, that's it.' She frowned. 'The station. Eagle's Ridge.'

'It was always Number One before.'

'Let's go back,' she said scrupulously moving away from him.

'I have to. There's work I've got to finish tonight.' He held her still for a moment looking down at her with a faintly bitter, self-mocking smile. 'You mattered, Laura, from the very first moment I saw you. I could have found every last thing about your devious plans but I would still have allowed you to come. Nothing seemed to matter. I simply—wanted you. I still want you and though you might fight me a little, you're mine.'

But that didn't settle anything. Several of the staff knew Laura's horse had returned riderless but Tait had left strict instructions no word was to be passed on to the house. Now that he had returned her safely, there was no need to say anything. Laura went back to the house as though nothing in any way unusual had happened, but for the life of her she couldn't eat very much at dinner.

She and Aunt Jessica were sitting quietly in the drawing room talking of this and that in their comfortable fashion when Philippa almost burst into the room.

'My dear!' Aunt Jessica looked up faintly alarmed. 'Is anything wrong?'

'Let me tell you, Aunt Jessica. Let me.'

In the perfumed warmth of the evening Laura suddenly felt ice-cold. Philippa was holding one of her foolscap folders, flipping rather wildly at the pages.

'Yes. Yes, of course.' Aunt Jessica was still staring at Philippa as though she had to humour a madwoman.

'Oh, I'm so sorry for you all,' Philippa cried gloatingly.

'My dear Mrs Hill,' Laura said in a cracking tone, 'unless I'm mistaken you're holding my private papers.'

'It's all here, Aunt Jessica,' Philippa cried. 'Stories about all of you. Articles she has written for that slimy magazine.'

'Rubbish!' Laura went to snatch the folder but Philippa clutched it frantically to her slight breasts. She was wearing blue tonight and the colour of her dress had picked up the unholy brilliance of her eyes. 'I assure you, Aunt Jessica,' Laura turned and spoke very directly to the older woman, 'Philippa is very wrong in her conclusions. I write to amuse myself. I always have done for as long as I can remember. It's natural for me to express myself on paper.'

'Oh, you liar!' Philippa cried. 'You're sending this to your magazine.'

'I haven't got a magazine,' Laura said curtly. 'I lost my job.'

'Please——' Aunt Jessica stared from one girl to the other. 'May I look at this, Laura?' she said.

'Certainly.' Laura had no objection to this fine writer seeing her work. 'It's all pretty much spontaneous, of course. I haven't worked over anything. My impressions, I suppose.'

Aunt Jessica took the folder without another word.

'Oh you sly creature!' Philippa gazed at Laura with the utmost contempt.

'Why don't you sit still and be quiet?'

It was far from the reaction Philippa expected. She did sit still for a moment in shock then she rallied. 'Oh, you deceitful thing!' She tore at the pearls at her throat. 'And to think the family trusted you. I told them. I told them, but they wouldn't be warned.'

'Philippa, please,' Aunt Jessica shook her head.

'You've made a mistake before,' Philippa told her. 'Remember how you liked and trusted that Maxwell girl? Beastly, beastly, thing!'

'Oh, Philippa.' Aunt Jessica lowered her head.

'Are you all right, Aunt Jessica?' Laura jumped up and went to the older woman's side, gently removing a hand so she could see into Aunt Jessica's face.

'Aunt Jessica!' Philippa spat out contemptuously.

At this point something snapped inside Laura. She flew up from the sofa and with superhuman strength bundled Philippa right out the door.

'Dear God!' Mrs Lambert, who was walking from the dining room to the kitchen stared at them transfixed.

'Aunt Jessica is not well,' Laura cried urgently. 'Get Tait.'

'Take your hands off me.' Philippa was burning with anger. 'How dare you? How dare you!'

'You say one more word and I'll hit you with that vase,' Laura's long fingers bit into Philippa's white skin. 'We're not concerned with you or me. Aunt Jessica cannot be subjected to stress.'

Philippa stared at her and Laura took a few steps backwards towards the vase. It would be a terrible thing to hit her. She was nonviolent and the vase was Ming dynasty.

'They'll blame you,' Philippa sneered. 'Tait will hate you for what you've done.'

Laura could see that she didn't mean to come back

into the drawing room so she flew back to Aunt Jessica.

'Laura, dear,' Aunt Jessica gasped and held out her arm.

'Oh, God!' Looking down at her Laura could see that Aunt Jessica was in pain. 'Tablets, your tablets?'

Aunt Jessica shook her head and Laura saw that there was sweat breaking out all over her face. 'Keep calm, now, calm. Tait is coming.' Very deftly Laura relaxed the frail body into a half-sitting, half-lying position. She was certain Aunt Jessica was having some kind of attack though the intense agitation seemed to be abating under Laura's tone. 'Tait's coming.' Please God, let him come. She was certain Aunt Jessica couldn't be shifted and she knew perfectly well how to give artificial respiration. Surely there was oxygen equipment in the house? In a remote station this size there was just about everything for urgent care.

She barely turned her head to look towards the door when Tait came racing in. Behind him was Mrs Lambert and behind her was the station foreman carrying oxygen equipment. This had to be a procedure they were used to, and Laura stepped aside quickly as Tait took control.

They sat with her all through the night: Tait on one side of the bed, Laura on the other with Lorne and Mrs Lambert hovering at intervals. Nobody spoke.

Why does it have to be like this? Why? Laura thought.

The breathing was very shallow and several times Tait got up to check, his jaw clamped tight.

He'll hate you for what you've done, Philippa had said. Poor, pitiful, vindictive Philippa. She thought she could endure his hatred to spare Aunt Jessica. Yet Aunt Jessica had not blamed her. She had clung to her for comfort, frail body jerking. Aunt Jessica was her friend. They had looked into each other's eyes.

Laura thought she had dozed for when she came round again an exquisite lemon glow emanated from the filmy curtains. She almost bounced up in her armchair staring towards the bed in fright.

'No more,' Tait's voice said. He was standing in deep shadow, though she could see the rigid line of his back and the glimmer of his pale shirt. 'My beloved aunt is no more.'

The shock took Laura's breath away; then she bowed her head and wept.

CHAPTER TEN

THEY came from everywhere for the funeral; a curious mixture of the very rich and the stunningly poor. The brown people walked in from the desert while their white brothers flew in in private planes.

'Is everyone going to die, Laura?' Jamie asked her fearfully and Laura was so concerned for him she got a steely hold on herself.

'Aunty Jessie wasn't well for a long time,' she explained to him. 'She wasn't young, Jamie, like you and I.'

'She wasn't old either,' Jamie said anxiously and remained glued to Laura's side.

Gradually the house emptied of visitors, relatives and close friends and it was time to return to a semblance of normal life. Laura and Tait had extraordinarily little to say to each other, but Lorne, for some reason Laura couldn't understand, suddenly attached himself to her as though things didn't hurt so much when she was around.

It was a very distressing time but what hurt the most was her remoteness from Tait. How could he not blame her? Innocent or guilty the end result had been the same. Wasn't that what Philippa wanted? To destroy Laura at any cost? Never mind who else was made to suffer. Of course her time at Eagle's Ridge was over, but in that first fortnight it was silently acknowledged her presence was very important to Jamie. There had been too much upheaval in his young life and it could not have been plainer that Lorne was ill-equipped by nature to play the all-important role of father. Even Jamie at five had come to accept his father did not think or feel or act like a proper father should. It was simply a matter of something vital left out.

Philippa had gone. Strange creature. She had become hysterical and Tait had lost little time persuading her parents to come and take her away. They had done so very promptly and with obvious misgivings. Philippa had been rather a problem in her adolescence but the late twenties had brought her to the full boil. Both of them anticipated having a truly hard time.

At first it upset Laura appallingly but then she decided she was going to find the ability and sheer guts to finish Aunt Jessica's work. The framework was all there and it was her only means of assuaging the sorrow that was in her. Aunt Jessica had been such a lovely woman. Her book demanded to be finished and perhaps, Laura thought, I can do it. It was an act of love and even if the publishers turned it away on the grounds that the concluding chapters hardly matched Jessica McEwan's inimitable style at least she had tried. For Aunt Jessica. Laura really felt she would get help.

Lorne, of course, continued to pay little attention to his son but then out of the blue he told them Laura's portrait was ready for viewing.

'Come along everybody,' he said.

Tait, looking hard and remote, suddenly flared into action, pushing away from the table and saying he would come at another time for the morning's muster required instructions to the men.

'What's wrong with Tait?' Lorne, so insensitive to others, looked deeply hurt and affronted.

'We all mourn in our own way,' Laura pointed out rather shortly. 'I think it's marvellous the way he keeps going.'

'Nevertheless I've never known him like that.'

Nor had Laura. Tait was already turning away from her. She didn't imagine she would be staying on at Eagle's Ridge. She would hate to leave Jamie. She always knew her devotion would come back to haunt her. Jamie wasn't her child. She had become much too fond of him; much too involved in his young life. Whether Lorne chose to leave him at Eagle's Ridge or not it could have little to do with her.

The paint was scarcely dry on the canvas and Laura stood silently for many moments before she felt she could advance an opinion. Lorne Sutton's tremendous panache was there. A beautiful woman was almost essential to his style but surely she wasn't as beautiful as that, or as sweet and dreamy. In fact, she wasn't a dreamy person at all. It was immensely decorative, she thought, but she felt at a total loss to come up with more than that.

'Well?' Lorne showed an uncharacteristic anxious modesty.

'It's beautiful—very beautiful, Lorne.' She didn't look directly at him.

'I knew you would like it,' he murmured, almost tenderly? Laura couldn't be sure. 'Just the same I was a little nervous—most unusual for me.'

'You're wonderfully gifted,' she said quietly. But not yet a great artist. Perhaps never. Yet the assurance was superb. Skin, eyes, hair glowed. Her young beauty radiated from a gauzy greyish-green background and he had painted the lace ruffle on her white dress with the utmost delicacy and precision. It was masterly in a way but Laura felt he had left out the essential characteristics of the sitter. The physical grace was all there but not the quickness or what she thought of as the vigour of her mind. It was quite obvious he didn't know her at all. There was nothing of Laura's undoubted resourcefulness in the eyes. But then her judgment wasn't impeccable. Others might see the portrait differently. Laura could only say it didn't express her.

She was standing so silently, so gravely, Lorne turned her to him with a sigh. 'My dear Laura, you must see from the portrait that I've come to care for you?'

She seemed to go rigid in every limb.

'You are the only one who has been able to make me

forget the misery of this past year.'

'Is your son nothing to you?' Laura suddenly cried. She couldn't even talk about Anne. She couldn't even believe it. Lorne Sutton interested in her? She had never even looked at him except as Jamie's errant father.

'I seem to have shocked you,' Lorne said slowly, the fire banking in his coal-black eyes.

'I see no reason why you wouldn't,' Laura managed carefully. 'I have always looked on you as Jamie's father—a man in deep mourning.'

'Which I was.' Lorne looked very faintly angry. 'I cared deeply about my wife—the accident almost made me lose my reason—but you've almost literally brought me back to life. I feel the excruciating days are over. I can work. I have hope, and obviously Jamie has taken to you tremendously. He has always been extraordinarily hostile to me. No, don't frown. The boy has never really liked me. He adored his mother. I sometimes think she fostered a dislike of me in him.'

'I can't believe that,' Laura said.

'Well, Laura, you don't know. Anne went ahead and married me despite McEwan opposition. I know they thought I was a disastrous choice but in the beginning she loved me madly. I do have a certain charm for a lot of women.'

Not me, Laura thought wildly. I don't really like you at all.

'I'm sorry I've startled you, but I would have you think of me in a different way. I've been drifting terribly I know, but that deep-down hopelessness has gone. I'm ready to go forward again—share my life with another woman.'

Laura shook her head and flushed deeply. 'I can't talk to you of this, Lorne.'

'You're so young.' He caught a thick skein of her hair and twisted it around his wrist. 'I blame myself for speaking out too quickly. But I must make a decision about Jamie. You seem to be very fond of him?'

'I love him,' Laura said plainly.

'Well——' There was a small silence. 'Surely I don't have to point out Jamie would miss you terribly if you went out of his life? And there's no need! In this last week or so I thought we'd grown close together. I can talk to you, Laura.'

God and I've barely listened, Laura thought.

'Jamie needs a mother,' Lorne said, 'and I'm absolutely certain I could teach you to love me.'

'No.' Laura shook her head. 'I can't allow you to hope . . .'

'You want time.'

'No, Lorne.' She felt so depleted the task of getting through to him was almost beyond her.

'You would have a good life with me,' he said. 'You would want for nothing.'

'I want for nothing now.'

'All women want to be married.' He looked down at her expectantly. 'You've made a sweeping change in my life, Laura. I can sort myself out with you and you can sort out Jamie. He quite exhausts me.'

By the time Laura reached her room her legs had almost given out under her. The whole thing was unbelievable. Lorne had lost his young wife in the most tragic circumstances, Aunt Jessica had scarcely been laid to rest and Lorne very calmly announces he was ready to entertain the idea of re-marriage. She was so astounded she didn't know what to do. Rant madly? Laura slumped down at the dressing table letting out a deep breath of air. For one terrible moment she had thought he was about to kiss her. She believed she would have screamed. How could a man convince himself a woman might be willing when she had never so much as glanced at him with anything else but pity and a general disapproval? Didn't he know she was disgusted by his lack of parental feeling? He really deserved Jamie's dislike and now that she thought about it Jamie wasn't under his father's spell. It was almost total incompatability.

Laura stared into her darkened, smoky eyes and to her horror burst out crying. There wasn't anyone she could talk to. No Tait. It was agonising.

The bout of crying, however short, she had to stop herself, left her headachey and sleepless. The little tension-relieving tricks she often practised all failed. She felt tremendously worried about Jamie. She had allowed the child to become very attached to her, yet how could she not have? He needed a kind woman—a mother substitute if you liked.

Around midnight she pulled on her robe and went downstairs. She had never seriously considered becoming a drinker, but a short something might put her to sleep. Daddy liked a whisky when things were difficult. In lots of ways she had had an intense life and a lot of worries for someone her age. It was terrible to feel profoundly alone.

She almost screamed when she walked straight into Tait and he seemed equally arrested.

'God, Laura, what are you doing wandering around in the dark?' His beautiful voice was filled with a hard impatience.

'Is it a sin?' she asked shortly. Why, oh why wouldn't he speak to her? She could hear the snap of his fine, white teeth.

'It could be. Believe it.'

'And what is that supposed to mean?'

'Are you sure you want to know?' He had almost caught her off the floor, now he let her go. 'I don't care for your portrait.'

'Have you seen it?' She gave a little, breathy gasp.

'Let's go and have another look.'

She recoiled a little, shocked at the bitter mockery of his tone, but he put one hand beneath her elbow and ushered her away to the room Lorne had been using as a studio.

'*Voilà—la belle* Laura!'

The room was plunged into brilliant light and she looked up at him wretchedly. Always honed to the bone he had a special tautness about him, a bitter mockery overlaid with tragic overtones. There was no doubt about it, Tait was suffering.

'Tait?' Because she loved him so much she put out her hand. It was an imploring hand but he appeared not to see it.

'I don't exactly think he has painted you.'

'No.' She couldn't help but agree.

'You don't like it?' He rounded on her, his green eyes as brilliant and oddly menacing as some jungle cat's.

She drew her soft yellow robe a little closer around her. 'It's excellent in its fashion.'

He laughed shortly. 'Did you tell him that?'

'I don't particularly like hurting people. Besides, he has a very large following. I could be wrong.'

'Well, fortunately, I'm not. There is such a thing as being extremely good without the likelihood of ever becoming great.'

'I wonder why he doesn't care about Jamie,' Laura said.

'He doesn't really care about anybody,' Tait returned very sombrely, 'unless he has suddenly decided to fall in love with you?'

'How the devil could he?' Laura cried miserably.

'Lorne is rather a shallow person, my dear Laura. I insisted he come here for Jamie's sake. Jamie, my sister's little son. The really terrible part was Anne only took a very short time to realise Lorne was—an actor, if you like. He adores admiration, adulation. He loves women for their beauty and God knows there's nothing wrong with that, but there has to be the woman, the human being you're closest to in all the world. Lorne never took the trouble to know my sister. Any more than he would ever take the trouble to know you.'

'I have no interest in Lorne, you know,' she said very quietly. 'I have a terrible headache, Tait. Do you think I might have a little drop of whisky or something to make me sleep?'

'Oh I'm sure we can do better than that.' He looked at her in a profoundly disturbing way. 'I can almost taste your skin in my mouth.'

She was breaking, she knew it. 'You've hardly said a word to me in weeks.'

'Well, why don't we crack a bottle together?' He laughed shortly and moved away from the portrait towards her.

'I feel for you, Tait,' she said. 'I feel very deeply for your hurt.'

'I know that,' he said briefly, though his handsome face was set in hard, proud lines. 'I should have thrown Philippa out months before I did. I always had the right instinct about her, but in a way she was such a pathetic creature. I know Jeff used to worry about her—worry what might happen to her if he wasn't around. My leniency has depressed me deeply.'

'You can't possibly blame yourself,' Laura said.

'Can't I?' He looked very remote and tall, staring down his straight nose at her. 'Well, Laura, are we going to get drunk or not?'

'I know I'm not.'

'You don't know what might happen to you yet.'

She wanted to retreat before the coiled tension of his tone but he took one more look at the portrait then groaning he turned off the light.

'So, shall we go in?' He paused at the door of his study.

'Tait?' She looked up at him with her lovely, luminous eyes.

'You can't be frightened of me, Laura.' He gave a derisive laugh. 'I have the control of ten men.'

'You drive yourself too hard.'

'So I do.' His faint chuckle was savage. 'Oh, come in for God's sake before I shake you.' He switched on the light and as she slipped past him his green eyes flashed. 'You've got thin.'

'So have you.' She moved to sit in one of the huge, black-leather armchairs. 'I think you should have a break, even if it's only a short one.'

'I might at that. One way or the other, Laura, you'll be the first one to know when it happens.'

'I'm not sure I can stay here any longer, Tait.' Her voice shook with emotion but instead of softening his aggression he all but snorted.

'Please, Laura, darling,' he said.

'I'm hurting as much as you are.'

'Are you, dear girl?' He poured whisky into two fat crystal glasses, splashed it with a little water and held one glass out to her. 'You must have the book finished by now.'

'Book?' There were tears in her eyes.

'Darling, I know what you've been slaving over all these long nights.'

'It's something I have to do, Tait,' she said. 'I have to do it. I'm going to do it.'

'Don't shout.'

She stared into the brilliant liquid. 'I loved Aunt Jessica.'

'Who didn't?'

'Tait, you sound so . . . hard and bitter.'

'But everything is so bitter.' He tossed his drink off. 'I failed to remove Philippa and I should have. I knew she was insanely jealous of you—us. Could anything be worse than having a woman you didn't want in love with you? No one else would take her in. Her parents these days would like to deny her existence.'

'Aunt Jessica wanted to help her too,' Laura pointed out, feeling the hot tears scald her eyes again. 'And Tait, her heart condition must have been serious.'

'A death sentence,' he said. 'She made Adams swear not to tell me just how bad she was.'

'And she loved you so much.'

'And what about you, Laura?' He laughed sardonically 'I haven't noticed your coming to my door to comfort me. You can't begin to know how much I wanted you or how lucky you were not to find me right beside your bed. I could have gathered you up.' He moved away to the sideboard and poured himself another drink. 'Drink up, Laura. You're a wash-out as a drinking partner.'

'I think this tastes like poison.'

'Continue drinking it and you won't.'

'All right.' She didn't stop until she had finished her portion.

'There,' he said softly, 'doesn't that burn?' His eyes were moving over her, her face, her breasts, her slender legs. 'You're never close to me now, Laura.'

'I thought you didn't want me. I thought you couldn't forgive me for my part.'

'I suppose if Jessie would forgive you, I can.'

The harshness of his tone robbed her of her frail control. She stared at him desperately for a moment, then flew up from the armchair. 'You can't hurt me any more. Do you hear?'

'You silly little fool!' He was on her before she had even reached the door, jerking her back into his arms. 'Hurt you. Hurt you. I want to devour you!'

She tried to lash out at him, her love perverted, but he pinioned her arms, crushing her back against the locked double doors. 'There's no help for you, Laura,' he said. 'There's only me.'

Behind the fierceness and the male dominance, there was still that look of suffering and though he brought his hand up hard beneath her jaw, Laura confounded him by lifting herself up on her tip-toes and staring deep into his eyes.

'I love you,' she said. 'I love you.'

'You can't play——'

'I want to stay with you forever.' She moved her body right into his so his arms almost involuntarily lost their appalling tautness and he began to cradle her.

'I've had this crazy longing—need—to come to you every night.'

'You could have.' Her silvery eyes were very direct. 'There is nothing I wouldn't give you. Nothing.' She tilted her blonde head forward so it lay against his breast. 'Oh my dear, darling, wretched Tait, won't you love me?'

'Laura?' He made her look at him and his hand moved over the naked curve of her breast. 'I can't let you go, little one. Don't ask me.'

'No.'

Very slowly he lifted her . . .

There was no one to watch them as he carried her up the stairs and it wouldn't have mattered greatly if there had been. Her slender body seemed to sink into the softness of the great bed and he gently locked the door and extinguished all the lights except for the two sconces that flanked the fireplace.

There was a moment when he held her shoulders and stared down into her face, one moment and no longer, but Laura understanding raised herself and kissed his mouth.

'Dear God, dear God,' he murmured very softly. 'My lovely Laura, I've wanted you so badly.' He was lowering her body gently back on to the bed and she pulled him down to her, returning his kisses so deeply that the last thread of his hard self-control snapped under the tremendous tension. He began to remove her soft robe, the thin nightdress, an exquisite reverent slowness in all his movements until her body was naked and crying out for his.

'You're so beautiful!' In his touch was all his love. He even seemed a little frightened of woman-magic.

'I want you,' she said very softly.

'I think I've wanted you since time began.' He lowered his head and put his mouth to her white, rose-capped breast.

There was silence. Long, long, minutes of silence, while he kissed and stroked and caressed her, exploring her beautiful body until her response was so urgent she was begging for the act of possession. She needed him desperately inside her, the act of love. And it was love. So perfect, so blazing, so mysterious, who could ever question that it was the greatest miracle on earth? She was consumed with the wonder of it, their longing for each other. She didn't know her cheeks were damp with tears.

'Oh, God, how I love you.'

'I love you too.'

It was all he allowed her to say for a long while.

'Tait?'

'Yes, my love?'

They were lying quietly, Laura turned sideways in his arms, his hand stroking her hair and her damp brow.

'What are we going to do about Jamie?'

'Are you thinking Lorne won't want him with him?'

'Will he?' She lifted her head a little to look into his face.

'No.'

She couldn't bear to say Lorne had all but proposed to her. It was so hurtful on so many counts.

'Can you take my little nephew on?' He held her face up and kissed her mouth. 'Of course, you have to marry me first.'

'Please. Quickly. It's very scary to love someone as much as I love you. As for Jamie—how could a father be so heartless?'

'Lots of children have lonely bitter years,' he said gravely. 'Some people don't have a lot of love to offer. Not like you, Laura, my beloved girl. I'll speak to Lorne. I'm just about ready to kick him out of my house.'

'What?' She looked at him in total amazement.

'Relax, darling.' He soothed her. 'I know all about Lorne. And his proclivities. I won't forget to tell him either that we're officially engaged as from now and we'll be married just as soon as I can arrange it. It's what you want isn't it?'

'How can you ask?' She sighed deeply and tightened her arms around him.

'Little virgin. Virgin no longer.' He lowered his

head. 'Does it matter?' His voice was very deep and tender.

'No.' She sighed voluptuously.

'Jess knew I loved you,' he said and smiled for the first time. 'I think she was very happy about that.'

'I know my parents would be very happy with you.' She held his head and kissed him. 'Nicky too. Family is so important.'

'Yes, darling.' His hands fondled her exquisite young breasts. 'I think I made love to you for the first time last night. It was quite a dream. I couldn't fight out of it.'

'And what about the reality?' She bent forward and kissed the cleft in his chin. There was a real question behind the smile in her eyes.

'The greatest wonder of my life!' His arms enfolded her strongly and he turned her so she was lying beneath him. 'I want you again,' he murmured urgently.

'I know.' The contractions in her body were answering his; a tremendous accumulation of sensation.

'My love. My sanity. My life.' He made it sound so simple yet so sacred.

She couldn't answer but simply lay looking up at him her soul in her eyes.

'Lovely Laura.' His voice was very quiet and his eyes roamed her face, the flawlessly textured skin. 'How's the headache now?'

'Gone.'

'You could say thank you.'

'Thank you.' It was pure, tortured pleasure, this tender teasing. She could feel her body come to violent, aching life.

He smiled, then something wrenching in her expression made him draw a quick breath. 'Darling, come with me,' he said harshly.

'Oh God . . . please.' She could feel the shaking start in her.

He held the back of her head with passionate intensity, then feverishly they returned to making love.

Perfect love. It existed.

You're invited to accept 4 books and a surprise gift Free!

Acceptance Card

Mail to: Harlequin Reader Service®

In the U.S.
2504 West Southern Ave.
Tempe, AZ 85282

In Canada
P.O. Box 2800, Postal Station A
5170 Yonge Street
Willowdale, Ontario M2N 6J3

YES! Please send me 4 free Harlequin Romance® novels and my free surprise gift. Then send me 6 brand new novels every month as they come off the presses. Bill me at the low price of $1.65 each ($1.75 in Canada)—an 11% saving off the retail price. There are no shipping, handling or other hidden costs. There is no minimum number of books I must purchase. I can always return a shipment and cancel at any time. Even if I never buy another book from Harlequin, the 4 free novels and the surprise gift are mine to keep forever.

116 BPR-BPGE

_____

Name   (PLEASE PRINT)

_____

Address   Apt. No.

_____

City   State/Prov.   Zip/Postal Code

This offer is limited to one order per household and not valid to present subscribers. Price is subject to change.   ACR-SUB-1

You're invited to accept 4 books and a surprise gift Free!

Acceptance Card

Mail to: **Harlequin Reader Service®**

In the U.S.
2504 West Southern Ave.
Tempe, AZ 85282

In Canada
P.O. Box 2800, Postal Station A
5170 Yonge Street
Willowdale, Ontario M2N 6J3

YES! Please send me 4 free Harlequin Presents® novels and my free surprise gift. Then send me 8 brand new novels every month as they come off the presses. Bill me at the low price of $1.75 each ($1.95 in Canada)—an 11% saving off the retail price. There are no shipping, handling or other hidden costs. There is no minimum number of books I must purchase. I can always return a shipment and cancel at any time. Even if I never buy another book from Harlequin, the 4 free novels and the surprise gift are mine to keep forever.

108 BPP-BPGE

_____
Name   (PLEASE PRINT)

_____
Address   Apt. No.

_____
City   State/Prov.   Zip/Postal Code

This offer is limited to one order per household and not valid to present subscribers. Price is subject to change.

ACP-SUB-1